A FAREWELL TO CHARMS

DOWN & DIRTY SUPERNATURAL CLEANING SERVICES BOOK 3

KATE KARYUS QUINN   DEMITRIA LUNETTA

MARLEY LYNN

For anyone who rolls their eyes when the word "literally" is used wrong - this book is for you.

CONTENTS

Sign up for our newsletter to receive FREE short stories!
Visit www.marleylynn.com/newsletter

Like us on Facebook for books deals, surprise sales, and promotions!
www.facebook.com/MarleyLynnAuthor

"Holy shit, am I dating the vampire serial killer?"

I wipe the vomit from my mouth as I hang out the side of my van and contemplate the life choices that brought me to this moment.

It all started with a guy. Of course it did.

But Liam was supposed to be a *nice* guy. And he seemed that way. Smart and funny and adorkable, with his cute British accent and board game parties. I ran to him for comfort after shit went down last week. And by comfort I mean sex.

Except he is such a gentleman that he didn't want to take advantage of me when I was clearly upset. So we just snuggled instead.

Yeah, he sounds too good to be true, which I guess in and of itself is a warning sign.

I lean back in my seat and rub the steering wheel. "Vanna, can you get me home please?" She honks her understanding and pulls out into traffic. With the state I'm in, she's a better driver than me right now.

Twelve years ago my normal minivan was stolen, then,

not too long ago, it showed back up on my doorstep with a mind of her own.

Needing to wash the puke taste out of my mouth, I climb into the back of the van where I keep a few bottles of water along with my cleaning supplies. I run my own business, a supernatural cleaning service, and it's important to stay hydrated while working all day scrubbing and dusting. Grabbing one of the waters, I fill my mouth and swish. Then rolling down the passenger window, I stick my head out and spit...

Right onto the police cruiser in the lane next to me.

The lady cop at the wheel turns to stare at me in shocked surprise. "Sorry," I yell as her gaze moves from me hanging out the back window, up to the empty driver's seat.

Her lights and siren come on.

Crap.

"Vanna, pull over," I say, as I scramble back into the driver's seat. It's too late to pretend anything is normal, so I let Vanna guide us to the side of the road while I dig in the glove box for the registration. By the time the cop comes up to the side window, I'm ready with a smile and my paper-work in hand.

"Morning, officer," I say.

She is not having it. "Do you know why you were pulled over?"

There is almost no chance that I'll get out of this without a ticket. But if I'm going to pay a giant fine, I at least want something to show for my money. So instead of answering, I ask a question of my own.

"Have you ever been unlucky in love? 'Cause I have been perpetually unlucky. First there was my ex-husband who turned out to be fae and a cheater. Then my almost fiancé who is so shady I can't even talk about him anymore because he made me sign a non-disclosure form. I mean, let's face it, most men are basically animals. And that's what I like about them. They're a little dangerous. A little wild. But I thought, okay Paige, that hasn't worked out, let's try someone a little more tame. That's when I met Liam, the supposed nice guy."

The officer sighs and I tense, wondering if this is the part where she drags me out of Vanna and pats me down looking for narcotics. But instead she nods and says, "You gotta watch out for the nice guys." She snorts derisively. "Those are always the biggest freaks."

"Yes!" I exclaim. "That's Liam exactly. Last night he was so sweet, but then this morning when he left to get us breakfast, I helped myself to his shower and some shampoo. Then I dug through his drawers, looking for a pair of sweatpants he'd promised me the night before. And that's when things went horribly wrong. I found a pile of photographs."

The cop smirks. "Porn, right?"

"You'd think. But no. Not porn. That would have been fine. I mean, Liam was single until he met me and guys are horny, even the nice ones. Porn would mean he's normal. Which is what I've been trying to be all my life."

"Girl…" The cop leans into the side window. "If you're going for normal, maybe try driving your own vehicle. Self-driving cars are not legal in New Jersey."

"Yes, officer, absolutely. You're right. It's just that Vanna isn't really a self-driving car, she's more of a self-driving…self."

The officer says nothing for a long moment, just gives me a long-suffering look. Finally, with a sigh she says, "You know, people like you are why I drink after work."

I nod, eagerly. "I get it. I'm sure you hear bullshit excuses all day long, but this van is sentient." I rub the steering wheel. "Say hello, Vanna."

She beeps twice.

The officer's eyebrows rise. "Trick horn?"

"No, I swear." I put up a few fingers in a formation that either means 'scout's honor' or 'rock and roll'—I always get those two confused. "Ask her a question. She's an incredibly responsive vehicle."

"All right," the officer says, looking amused. "I guess if vampires and werewolves are real, Herbie here is real too." She leans in the window and talks at the steering wheel. "Vanna, is your owner always a total flake, or is she really just having a bad morning?"

There's total silence which I hope means that Vanna is contemplating the question and not hanging me out to dry. Then suddenly the radio blares to life. I immediately recognize the chorus to Cypress Hill's "Insane in the Brain." As those words play over and over, I slap at the radio button, trying to turn it off.

"Okay, Vanna, that's enough. I think she gets it."

Finally the music cuts out and I look over to see the officer...laughing. Shaking her head and wiping tears from her eyes, she says, "Okay crazy girl, so tell me the rest of your story. What did the nice guy have in his drawer if it wasn't porn?"

I swallow hard, remembering the picture.

It featured Liam proudly holding a severed head. He gripped the hair and cheesed at the camera like he was displaying a trophy. The room he was standing in had more like it all around. A stuffed griffin. A manticore head mounted on the wall. And looking closer, there was even what looked like a werewolf pelt on the floor at his feet.

But the worst part was that the wall behind Liam was

entirely lined with fangs—vampire fangs. Hundreds of them.

The reason I rushed into Liam's waiting arms was because I'd just shot a vampire. He was in my house, ready to attack. Or so I thought. It was only after he was dead that I saw the gaping holes in his gums—black, bloodied pits where his teeth had been.

That photo and the wall of fangs tied Liam directly to VSK — the vampire serial killer who's been hunting in the supe community...and who seems to think we share a bond. He'd left that last vamp defanged and prepped for me to kill.

But I can't tell this cop that. The last time I sent a guy to the cops, he made the evidence disappear and got away easily. That's not gonna happen again. If Liam is VSK, I'm gonna make sure the evidence is airtight so that he's sent to jail for the rest of his life.

But now, of course, she's waiting for me to say something. I clear my throat and say the first thing that comes to mind, "Rooster shifter. There was a pic of him with wings and the big tail and even the wattle thing, but the rest of him was human form still so I could tell it was him. Of course I got the fuck out of Liam's apartment as soon as I found that photo. I ran. Ran away from everything that photo implied."

I wait for her to call me out on this big fat lie. Instead, she leans even further into my open window and pats my hand. "Aw girlfriend, it happened to me too. Same thing. My rooster shifter told me he was a honey badger shifter, which I don't think actually exists, but who knows, right?"

I nod even though I don't know why anyone would hear "honey badger shifter" and not run in the other direction.

"What did your supposed nice guy tell you he was?"

I open my mouth to say, "tour guide" and then realize that she thinks I wanted to be with a shifter, just not a *rooster* shifter. I run back through my words trying to think what might have given her that impression. It must've been when I said all men are animals—and that I wanted someone more tame. She didn't think, "Former English major loves her metaphors," but instead took my words literally.

Now I try to think of a tame animal that I'd want to fuck. I mean, if he was in human form. I draw a complete blank, but the cop is waiting for an answer so I say, "Box turtle."

Her eyebrows climb so high they're close to jumping right off her head.

"He wooed me with the story of the turtle and the hare," I quickly add. "You know the whole slow and steady wins the race. But in this case, he meant sex. I thought it'd be a great change to be with a guy who doesn't rush. But then I saw the chicken picture and…"

I shrug helplessly as I run out of bullshit.

But the cop buys it, 'cause she nods knowingly. "Same same same," she says. "Although mine was less of a nice guy. Also despite all of his cock-a-doodle-doo, sadly there was not a whole lot of actual cock to back it up." She holds two fingers a couple inches apart. "Hard he was this big. It was sad."

"Wow," I say, because what else can I say?

She nods. "Yeah, well, they can't all be hung like a bear shifter. Not that I've ever been with a bear. It's on my bucket list. I want to check off all the big game animals. So far I've got lion, jaguar, and a guy who told me he was a wolf, but in retrospect I think he was just a really hairy human."

I blink at her. "That's…" I try to think of a nice way to tell her that I try to *not* screw supes. There's no good way to say that, so I simply smile and offer, "I work at Charms. As the cleaning lady," I quickly add. "Is that where you, um, meet these guys, or er, girl shifters?"

She laughs. "Naw, I'm into dudes. And I know Charms, but I'd never go there. I like the thrill of the hunt. You know what I mean?"

I really, really don't. But I just smile.

"I'm Officer Esposito," she says, giving me her hand. "Angelina Esposito."

"Paige Harper," I answer, as we shake.

"You know, it's not every day I meet someone who has the same...taste in men." She gives me a conspiratorial wink. "We should go out to the bars together some night. Help each other cockblock so neither of us accidentally goes home with a rooster."

"That sounds great," I lie.

Officer Esposito gives me her card and we make loose plans for the coming weekend—apparently Big Game is a known shifter bar in town and she thinks we could do well there. Before leaving, she reminds me to stay in the driver's seat and at least try to look like I'm doing the driving.

I sag in my seat as Officer Angelina Esposito merges into traffic and disappears down the road.

I might've gotten myself out of a ticket, but it's totally possible I got myself into something way worse—a friendship with a total wingnut.

2

I get the first text from Liam as I arrive home.

Where did you go? I have breakfast.

Crap, what do I say? I don't want him to know that I'm on to him. I don't want to piss him off.

With shaky hands I type, *Work emergency. Big clean up. I need the money. Sorry for leaving!* Then I put a sad face.

No worries, as long as you're not ghosting me! Comes his immediate response. Then a ghost emoji. Then a smiley face.

I write, *LOL. Be in touch soon!* And hope I seem normal. At least you can't convey tone via text so Liam won't be able to tell I'm terrified.

I'm walking up the front steps when I spot the large box in front of the door. I freeze, hackles up. Automatically my hand moves to rest on the gun in the butt of my jean shorts.

I snatch my hand away like my fingers are burning.

The last time I reached for my gun—I shot someone.

Maybe he wasn't human anymore. And maybe he wasn't such a great guy even when he was human. But he didn't deserve to die.

I hate knowing I took a life. And I hate VSK for making me do it.

VSK started his weird flirtation with me by killing my neighbor's cat, TomTom Petty, and leaving him on my front porch; a crime I originally pinned on my ex, Brent. Then VSK upped the stakes by leaving me a note. In typical serial killer fashion the note was attached to the body of a dead vamp. Talk about a big gesture, right? It wasn't just any vamp either. This was the body of a vamp who wouldn't take no for an answer at a straw party...the same party where I'd met Liam.

Later, VSK attacked my enemies—leaving Giselle, my ex-boyfriend's current girlfriend, in a pile in the road and offering to do more. All I had to do was ask.

Of course I didn't ask. I don't want my enemies bleeding out on my doorstep. I want them always stuck in the slowest moving line at the grocery store. I want their internet to go out when they're in the middle of a Netflix streaming marathon. I want them to accidentally drop their phone into a gas station toilet. You know, normal petty bullshit that makes their lives miserable...and long.

My initial fear reaction is overrun by my anger. VSK—who might be Liam—has left something else on my doorstep. He thinks he can just deliver dead bodies, defanged vampires, and whatever is in this box—probably a corpse head, at the rate I'm going.

Well, fuck him. I'm done.

I mean, I didn't even get laid last night.

"Eat this!" I scream, and kick the box out of the way.

It yelps.

I scramble backwards, clawing at the door frame for balance. By the sound of it, I just kicked a puppy.

Nice. Great move, Paige Harper.

Even the Humans First—an anti-supe movement that has been known to resort to violence—wouldn't approve of my actions. The box is shaking, and a low, tense growl is coming from it as I approach. Gingerly, I reach out and snatch the note off the top.

Paige,

I can't always be around. It's time for you to have a guard dog. A real one.

He doesn't sign off, but he doesn't have to.

It's from Nico, the one-eyed werewolf private detective who rents the office space next to mine. He's been watching my property without my knowledge, skulking around in wolf form. Tracking down VSK is his case. I guess someone got sick of the cops having no clue—or no interest—in finding the guy.

Nico claims he got a good sniff of VSK the night Giselle was dumped in the street, tressed up and ready for slaughter, but that's the only clue we have to VSK's identity.

I'm going to have to tell Nico about the photo at Liam's, but first...

I peel back one of the cardboard flaps, trying to coo in a comforting tone as the growling kicks it up a notch.

"Hey there, little buddy," I say, when a pair of eyes meet mine. "What's your na—SHIT!!"

Our introductions are cut short as it leaps for my throat, supple body tearing through the cardboard. It's a blur of black and white and I smack at it, sending the puppy flying and bouncing off the side of the house.

"Nico, you son of a bitch," I mutter to myself. Tucking my gun back into my pants, I grab my phone instead.

"Eye Wide Open Private Investigations, Nico Tralano

speaking," he answers on the first ring, his low, assured voice in contrast to mine as I shriek.

"You gifted me a goddamn Dalmanther!"

The breed—new to the world ever since a species-curious panther shifter mated with a Dalmatian—is infamous. They're beautiful monsters, dog-cats with spots who are best known for killing their owners in return for the smallest infractions, like for example, serving room temperature water.

Nico's chuckle over the phone infuriates me more, as the puppy flips over in the grass, spots me, and begins wagging its tail furiously. I back away as it climbs the steps, but its head is down and its tail is between his legs. His upper lip is curled but he's dragging himself on his belly by the time he reaches the porch.

"Congratulations, you're a mother," Nico says.

"I'm definitely not," I snap. "The damn thing just tried to kill me."

Except...now it's being sweet. The puppy nudges against my knee, and looks up with imploring eyes.

"But you're not dead," Nico opines. "You must have shown it that you're the alpha. With your personality, I had no doubts that you would."

"Well...I kicked it and then threw it against the side of the house," I admit. Then add, "And what do you mean 'with my personality?'"

"Good," Nico says. "You just established dominance; he'll be loyal to you forever now. He's exactly what you need to stay safe from VSK."

The puppy whines, begging me for attention. I reach down hesitatingly to scratch his ear. It feels like velvet under my touch, but the warm spray of piss that splashes across my feet destroys the moment.

"Ugh, he just peed on me," I tell Nico.

"Yeah, that's called submissive urination," Nico—conversant in all things canine—explains. "That'll happen."

"Nice. Thanks again for this gift I didn't ask for that tried to kill me and is now going to piss all over my home."

"Don't forget he also needs special food. He will not accept generic grocery store puppy chow."

I groan, wondering how exactly I'm supposed to afford that.

"You're welcome," he says easily. "What'd you name him?"

"Nothing yet," I say, reaching down again as the puppy presses against my legs, tail switching back and forth.

"Choose wisely," Nico tells me. "They're an incredibly smart breed. They'll latch onto the first loud word they hear from the owner they've imprinted on. Make sure you say something that—"

But it's too late. I already screamed something at the Dalmanther puppy. "Oh no," I say, eyeing the bundle of warmth as I bend down, arms out.

"C'mere...c'mere..." Oh God, seriously? "C'mere, Shit."

The puppy goes wild, jumping into my arms and rubbing himself all over me. Even though I drop my phone, I can still hear Nico laughing.

"You had no right...," I seethe, grabbing my phone and hanging up on Nico while Shit wiggles in my arms. I'll eventually have to talk to Nico about Liam possibly maybe being VSK, but now is not the time.

I do a crazy balancing act—warm Shit, phone ringing with another incoming call, keys jangling in my shaking hands—as I push my shoulder into the door and stumble into the foyer. Shit hits the ground running and zooms into the living room. Darron's shriek is immediately followed by a massive crash.

"No!" I yell, following Shit's trail. I find Darron standing on the chair, holding a hand-embroidered pillow out of Shit's reach...which is pretty difficult. The puppy is launching himself off the ground, hindquarters coiled like a cat's, as he leaps for the pillow.

Shit has been in this room for thirty seconds, and already shredded a seat cushion and apparently head-butted the television. It lies in a pile of broken glass and fritzing out cords.

"Again?" I ask, eyes meeting Darron's. This is our third TV since he moved in. My mouth goes into a thin line. I'm making Nico buy the fourth one.

"SHIT, SIT!" I scream, and he immediately obeys, eyes locked on mine and muscles quivering in anticipation as pillow feathers fall softly all around him.

"What in the actual hell?" Darron asks. "We own a Dalmanther now?"

"Apparently," I mutter.

"And his name is Shit?" Darron follows up.

"Apparently," I say again, as I notice Shauna asleep on the couch. The commotion hasn't woken her up. She looks like hell, but I can't summon up a lot of sympathy for her. She recently promised to quit her drug of choice—beauty—so that she can be a good aunt to the vampire baby I'd helped rescue. But it looks like she spent the night partying with the beautiful people.

"How long has she been asleep?" I ask Darron, who is still on the chair, with Shit nipping at his feet.

"Since last night. She came back really stoned and passed out."

"Shauna. Wake up." I shake her hard. As a hybrid, part

vampire and part Fae, she can sleep, but only when she overdoes the beauty. Too much and she could end up in a coma from which she'll never wake.

Shauna shuffles a little and moans, throwing herself over the end of the couch, her pink hair streaming around her. Shit looks at me, his back end wiggling like a bowl of Jell-O. She lands on the floor and begins to snore. Shit walks over to her, lifts his leg, and pisses right on her feet.

"No," I say to him, sternly. He stops quivering, but he's still eyeing Shauna's hair in a way I don't like. If he gets hold of her, she's as good as scalped.

I'm the alpha. "Look, you little shit," I rail at the puppy. "No pissing in the house. No biting in the house. No...anything else destructive in the house."

He looks up at me with those puppy dog eyes and I want to melt and pick him up for a cuddle. But I stay strong and fold my arms. Shit bows down, lays down, then rolls on his back, submissively.

"That's a good boy," I tell him. I lean down and rub his belly while Darron steps off the chair.

"Why did you buy a puppy...kitten...thing?" he asks.

"I didn't buy him, judgey. He was a gift, and he's a Dalmanther."

Darron surveys the destruction. "Worst. Gift. Ever. And that's saying a lot around here. At least the thing is alive."

"Tell that to Nico," I mutter, still rubbing Shit's belly. He's cute as hell and despite myself I have to admit I'm falling in love with the little guy.

"That sexy one-eyed werewolf definitely wants to get into your jean shorts," Darron tells me. He comes a little closer and Shit rolls upright, sniffs Darron's shoes, then raises his leg.

"Don't you dare," I tell Shit, and he lowers his leg again,

his face all sweetness. He runs over to the pile of pillows strewn across the floor, takes a running leap, and lands center. Cuddling in, he watches me.

Darron and I clean Shauna up and get her back on the couch. She's barely five feet and weighs next to nothing. She looks so small and pathetic.

"We really have to do something about this," I tell Darron.

"I know. She wants to stop but she's in a lot of pain emotionally."

"Who isn't?" I ask. "My whole life is emotional pain. And I don't spend it doing drugs. I haven't been high since..." I stutter to a stop, not able to remember the last time I was high, or even drunk.

"There was that time you accidentally drank incubus sperm," Darron says helpfully.

"That was different," I tell him. "I was not high. I was just...easily orgasmic. And in my defense, I was wearing very tight jeans," I say. "And this conversation is over." I rub my eyes.

"Headache?" Darron asks, eyeing me with concern.

"No, just a life-ache," I tell him. A whimper comes from the pile of pillows on the floor and Shit jumps into my lap, delicately licking my face. When a tear slips out of one eye, he reaches a paw up, and touches my shoulder.

"Aww, thanks, little guy," I say, scratching his shoulder. "I'd love to sit around all day cuddling with you, but I've got a phone call to make." Shit hops down, letting me get out of the chair. I turn to Darron. "Let me know as soon as she wakes. We need to make her understand she can't keep doing this."

Darron crosses his arms. "You haven't dealt with a lot of addicts, have you?"

"Well, Jax was addicted to acting like a dick. Does that count?"

He shakes his head. "I think we need to go full on intervention with this one."

I nod. "Can you organize that?"

He sighs. "I have a lot going on too. I'm not your magical best friend queer who is always there and lives only to help you," he tells me.

"I know you're not," I promise him. "I know you have your own life. You're just better at the Shauna stuff, and the nurturing stuff, and pretty much all the stuff."

He tilts his head and raises his eyebrows. "Pleeeease?" I add.

He smiles. "Fine. Flattery will get you everywhere."

"Thanks, Darron. I really do appreciate all you do. I mean, when you first moved in, I had my doubts, but now I have no idea how life would be without you."

"Awwww," he gives me a hug. "Us girls have to stick together."

I give Darron a squeeze, then head up to my room. Shit follows me. Watching him get up the stairs brings a bit of joy, his puppy body taking each one like he's scaling Mount Everest. By the time we make it up to the attic, he's pooped. Not literally, thankfully. He leaps gracefully onto the bed and burrows under the covers.

Truth is, I'd love to follow his lead. I want nothing more than a nap. But I've got work to do, and as usual, it has zero to do with my actual job.

I hit a number and my cop friend picks up immediately. Not my new cop friend, horny-for-shifters Angelina Esposito. But my old reliable one.

"Hey Kiddo, what's up?" he asks.

My throat tightens. My parents are gone and I miss them

so bad it hurts. That's one reason I lean on Darron so hard; he's one of the few people in my life who I can rely on. Luckily, I've also become close with a detective who's helped me out more than once and is protective enough that I'm ready to dub him an honorary uncle—something I've never had since both my parents are only children.

"McGinnis," I say, "you know that background check you promised to do on Liam? Yeah, I'm gonna need that ASAP."

I fill him in on the shitshow that is my life, which takes less time than I thought it would.

I end up with the oddest feeling—I'm either the most interesting person in the world, or the most basic of all bitches.

3

I don't know what to do with Shit while I'm working so I take him to a Doggie Daycare. He really does just look like a normal puppy, a Dalmatian mix, so the cheerful woman working there doesn't even bat an eye. I tell her that he's a handful, but she just grins. "All puppies are!"

I also tell her to bill Nico at his office. He gifted me this adorable bundle of destructive cuteness. He can pay for the dog sitter.

I get to Charms and dig in. Charms is your friendly neighborhood supernatural brothel and gaming den. I have a weekly commitment to give it a good scrubbing. But it's turned into two or three times a week. I'm going to have to ask Canwella for more money for all the work I'm doing. It doesn't help that she's one of my few current paying customers so I don't want her to get rid of me for being too expensive.

Cleaning seems tedious to a lot of people and they'll do anything to get out of doing it, but I enjoy it. It lets my mind wander while I make the world a slightly better place. I always get such a feeling of accomplishment when I take a mess and scrub it into oblivion.

When I walk into the *Splash* room and find a creature chilling in the hot tub—but not the one I expect. Seraphina, the mermaid occupant, is usually lounging in one of the pools, or lying naked on the tile. I desperately try to be aware of when the staff is entertaining, and today is definitely Seraphina's day off. One of the hazards of the job is walking in on some truly kinky stuff. But this creature isn't a patron looking to get their jollies off by living a mermaid fantasy. It's the owner's nineteen year-old daughter.

"Oh. Hey...Romiette?" I say. She and her mother are ogres, and everything about them is large and bulbous. She turns her knobby head toward me. "We met a few weeks ago."

"Just call me Romy," she says. "You're that human cleaner my mom hired?"

I nod. Just like her mother, her voice is the only non-hideous thing about her. It's light and lyrical and I could listen to her speak all day.

"Yeah, but I can come back..."

"No, I'm not even supposed to be in here, but I couldn't resist using Seraphina's tub while she's out. That, like, literally never happens."

I hesitate, wondering if I can resist giving the girl an English lesson. Especially since I know what Romy means.

Usually Seraphina is in her room when I'm cleaning it. She likes to helpfully point out places I've missed. According to Canwella, she rarely leaves her room and almost never leaves Charms itself. Apparently, she was raised in captivity by some psycho collector of rare things and it left her with a raging case of agoraphobia.

Still, I really can't let such an egregiously wrong use of *literally* happen on my watch.

"It literally does happen," I correct as gently as I can. "Otherwise she'd be here right now."

Romy rolls her eyes, which is pretty much the response I was expecting. "You know what I mean, she's afraid to go out. But the last few days she's been reading this self-help blog or something and today she announced at breakfast that she was gonna swim laps at the YMCA." Romy dunks her head into the water and then comes back up, giving it a generous shake. "Anyway, now that you're here, I can get out of your way if you want."

"You're fine," I tell her as I wheel the cart into the room and get my mop ready. "What are you hiding from?" I ask.

"Who says I'm hiding?" Romy demands.

I laugh. "Come on, I clean your room too. Your tub is very generously sized."

"Yeah, but it doesn't have the jets," Romy mutters and I think that's the end of that when she adds. "It's just...everything," she motions vaguely. "My mother has been on my ass about taking over the business."

"You're not interested?" I ask. My own business is one I started with my dad. Both my parents disappeared in the Great Ghosting two years ago, when a bunch of people just up and vanished into thin air.

"I don't want to do what she does. I want to do my own thing. Soaking in the hot tub, it gives me time to think." She adjusts herself; her large breasts float up to the surface of the water looking like green mountain islands. I avert my gaze but not before getting an eyeful of the butterfly tramp stamp on her lower back.

"Canwella seems to be a fair person," I start. "Maybe if you just talk to her..."

Romy rolls her eyes. "Yeah, she seems nice and fair, unless she's given birth to you." She sinks down into the water. "Hey, can I borrow that?" she motions to one of my scrub brushes.

"Sure, but I use this to get the algae off the tile," I tell her as I hand it over. "It's a very rough bristle."

"Perfect!" she says as she uses it to scrub her armpits. Her face softens. "Oh yeah, that's the spot."

My phone buzzes in my pocket and I take it out. It's McGinnis, finally calling me back. "I have to take this," I tell Romy. "You won't tell your mom that I'm on my phone during company time?"

Romy laughs, and it's so musical it makes me smile. "As long as you don't tell her I'm hiding in here."

"Deal!" I say and step into the bathroom. Since the *Splash* room is a hot tub, a small pool, and a fountain, this room is tiny and only has a sink and toilet. I put down the toilet lid and have a seat.

"McGinnis, what did you find?" I ask.

His strong voice washes over me, and it's comforting, despite his message not being the one I wanted. "It's not good news kiddo, I'm sorry."

My heart drops into the toilet. "Liam is…" I can't even say it.

"Squeaky clean. Not so much as a parking ticket since he moved to the States five years ago."

"How is that bad news?" I ask.

"Liam's father is doing time in the UK for murder."

My mouth drops open. "Who did he murder?"

"The better question would be, who *didn't* he murder? He was a notorious vampire killer. But he wasn't picky. He'd also kill any other kind of supe he came across. In the end, no one is sure exactly how many supes this guy disposed of.

About ten years ago when all the supernatural creatures came out of the closet, things were crazy. The weather, earthquakes, there was even a rumor that NYC fell into the ocean."

"I remember," I say. I was in my early twenties, just starting out in the cleaning business with my dad. The east coast was sketchy, but I know other parts of the country and the world were hit really hard. It was a bona fide apocalypse.

"Well, if you think things are iffy legally with supes now, back then it was like the wild west. This guy killed hundreds of supes, and the authorities didn't arrest him because they didn't know if supes counted as people or not."

"That's messed up. But wait, how is he in jail now?"

"Because the idiot managed to kill someone who was only pretending to be a vampire. He staked some goth girl and went down for murder."

"Do you have a picture of the dad?"

"Sure, hold on," McGinnis tells me and I hear him fiddling around with papers, then snapping a photo, then muttering to himself about stupid smart phones. Despite the grim conversation, I smile. He reminds me so much of my dad.

I look at the pic he just sent, a mug shot, and almost drop my phone. "That's Liam's dad?" I ask. "It looks just like him." There are a few differences, but at a quick glance they're a dead ringer for each other. "The creepy photo I found at Liam's could be of his dad?" I'm a mix of emotions: fear, anger, hope, relief. I don't know what to think.

"I can't say, Paige. Did you take the photo from his house, or snap a picture of it?"

"No, I just got the hell out of there," I tell him.

"Smart girl. Better safe than sorry."

"No, I ran like a coward," I say.

"You were being cautious. That's not cowardly."

"So, Liam might be following in dear old daddy's footsteps? Or he might just be unfortunate in his bloodline. I mean, we can't choose our parents." Which doesn't explain why he'd keep the pics of his dad and the supe kills, but I'm grasping at any straws that could mean Liam really is what I need him to be—a good guy.

"You stay away from that sonofabitch until I can find out more," McGinnis says. "I'll figure out his routine and search his apartment when he's out. Might take me some time 'cause it will have to be off the books. There's no way I could get a warrant on you saying you saw a photo. Do you know his work schedule?"

"I think it changes a lot. He runs tours for a supe tourist company." God, like that wasn't a red flag. My mind races. "I could get him out of his apartment, go on a date with him. Text you when we're out and when we're coming back. Then you'd know you were safe."

"You're the one who needs to be safe, Paige. There's no way I'm letting you do that."

"I appreciate that, McGinnis, but I'm a big girl and I know how to handle myself. We'll drive separately and meet in a public place. I'll have my phone and gun on me at all times."

He sighs heavily. "I don't like it, Paige. You're a good kid but you've got a real knack for finding trouble. I hate that you're always having to deal with these assholes. Murdering vampires, that nasty ex of yours, and even that dumbass with the pregnant vamp wife."

"Yeah, lots of shit rolls up on my doorstep. Which reminds me, I've now got a little extra help with security at the house. A friend gifted me a Dalmanther puppy."

There's a long pause and then a shaky laugh. "Paige, my

hearing must be going. I could've sworn you just said someone gave you a Dalmanther."

"No, that's what I said. He was on my porch this morning. Scared the hell out of me and that's why he's now named Shit."

"Who the hell would leave a Dalmanther like that? People have had their throats ripped out by those *things*. And they don't have to be big to be lethal, either."

McGinnis sounds pissed now, like he's ready to go out and throw someone behind bars.

"It's okay," I say, trying to calm him down. "It all worked out."

"Was it Liam?" he asks, refusing to let it go.

"No, of course not. He's way too responsible to do something like that."

"That ex-boyfriend of yours? The one that tried to kill you? Or his nasty new girlfriend—the redhead?"

"No and no. Also—"

Before I can steer this conversation McGinnis goes on. "One of your roommates then? The faerie? Or the *other* fairy? The guy/gal."

"No," I say again, my tone harder this time.

There's a sinking feeling in my gut as I realize just exactly how much my life has strayed from where I imagined it would be. I was pretty anti-supe after my divorce, but hearing everything come out of his mouth, I sound like a real sympathizer.

Still...I don't like his tone right now. And he doesn't really know these people. Especially Darron.

"It's that Nico, the P.I.," McGinnis concludes. He is a detective after all. "He gave you the monster."

"Enough!" I snap. "Yeah, it's true, I've had bad luck and maybe even worse taste when it comes to picking romantic partners. But my friends are the best. They are not suspects and they have not hurt me."

There's a long silence on the other end of the phone and I wonder if I just ended my relationship with McGinnis. But then he sighs heavily and says, "You're right. I overstepped. I'm sorry." Another sigh and then he adds, "You still okay with counting me among those friends?"

"Of course," I say instantly, relieved this didn't turn into more of a thing. "And I'll be careful with Liam," I promise. "But I gotta do this. I gotta know the truth about Liam or else it's gonna make me crazy."

"Well, I'm not your father, Paige, though you have definitely grown on me these last months. I care about you."

My eyes start to tear up a bit. McGinnis is a good man. Someone I can trust. Sure, maybe he was a little overbearing for a minute there, but it's just because he cares. And it's not his fault he's old school. He was walking a beat long before supes were a part of our world. This life changed just as much as everyone else's did; I'm just young enough to pivot faster. "I care about you too."

"And I know that you're very capable of defending yourself, if you want to do this. As long as you're out in public, I'm sure you'll be okay."

"Then I'll set up a date and let you know when he'll be out."

"Okay, kiddo, just be careful. And don't forget to bring your gun loaded and ready, just in case."

"I never leave home without it," I assure him even though I can't stop myself from once again flashing back to pulling my trigger and hitting another living creature. There's no reason to share that with McGinnis, though.

After I hang up with McGinnis I wash my face and dry my sweaty hands. My life can't possibly be any worse, I think as head downstairs to the gambling rooms. I need a break, maybe a cuddle with Shit.

As I step onto the stairs, though, I realize something is very wrong. At the card table all the players are slumped in their chairs, passed out cold. I'm wondering if this is some sort of practical joke when I catch sight of a man in a mask with a gun in one hand and a duffel bag in the other. Hundred-dollar bills flutter to the floor around him.

Our eyes meet and hold. I swallow hard, realizing it's too late for me to find cover. Deciding to brazen it out, I put my hands on my hips. "You better not think I'm cleaning up this mess," I say.

Apparently the dude is not a fan of sassy cleaning ladies.

He points the gun at me and fires.

4

I'd like to say my whole life flashes before my eyes, but the trite thing I think about is that I never finished scrubbing the *Splash* room and Seraphina is going to complain to Canwella about the algae build up.

I blink. I'm still standing. No blood, no bullet hole. I let out a shaky breath and stare down the robber. He doesn't have a normal gun; it's a magical supe stun gun. Brent, my shitbird ex-boyfriend, has the same kind. It only affects supes.

"You're human?" the masked man asks, confused.

"You bet your ass I am. And this is a real-ass human gun," I say, pulling out the gun I always keep tucked into the back of my pants. I click off the safety. "Put down the money and kneel on the floor." If he's using a stun gun, that means no one should be dead, but they'll be out for quite a while.

I can tie him up and...

"What's going on?" Romy asks as she barrels down the stairs. She takes in the masked gunman. "Holy Hades, are we being robbed?"

"Yes, watch his stun gun—"

Romy is a big girl, and once that bulk gets moving, it's hard for her to stop. She runs into me and knocks me on my ass, sending my shot wild and the gun flying across the floor.

"Shit!" I scramble for it, but the masked man picks up his bundle of money and is out the door. Romy follows him. That girl is going to get herself stunned, or worse.

I grab the gun and chase after her; she's running down the street after a car, which must be the getaway vehicle. Charms is located in a normal suburban neighborhood, and looks just like any other house. I wonder what the neighbors will think of a giant ogress running down the street? There's no way she's going to catch that car.

Canwella appears at my side. "Romiette!" she shouts, her voice blasting down the street. "Get back here this instant!"

I think she's concerned for her daughter's safety, but when she comes huffing and puffing back to Charms, Romy gets a scolding. "What are you doing running down the street like a crazed monster?" She pulls us both back inside. "Our neighbors are going to complain."

"I thought I could catch them," Romy says.

"Should I call the police?" I ask. "I know a good one…" After I told McGinnis off, now is probably not the time to ask for more favors, so I'm a little relieved when she shakes her head.

"No cops," Canwella tells me. She surveys the games room. All her patrons are out cold.

She wheels on us. "Did you see who it was? Did you see how many?"

"I only saw one," I start. "It was a man, but he was wearing a mask."

"There were more in the car," Romy tells her.

"Did you get the license number?" she asks, but Romy only shakes her head.

"Okay, they got the gaming money, but at least they couldn't get into the safe."

"Have you checked it?" Romy asks.

"No, but it's the best I could find, locked with spells."

Romy and I exchange a glance. "The guy had a magical stun gun," I tell her. "Whoever they are, they came prepared for supes."

Canwella's face drops and she hurries to her office, with me and Romy hot on her heels. We burst in to find it in disarray. Papers everywhere and standing with the door wide open...her safe.

Canwella sinks to the ground. "We're ruined," she says.

Romy goes to her. "Mom, it's okay. We'll make the money back. Things will just be tight for a while."

"No, you don't understand. All that money...it was everything I had. Employee salaries and the mortgage. All the money I've made over the last five years was in that safe. And it's time to pay off the homeowners and the cops and the city."

"You bribe all those people to keep Charms operating?" I ask.

"If we don't get that money back, Charms is going to close down," she wails.

I sigh, right an overturned chair and sit down. Even though I know better than to say it aloud, I can't help but think that my raise is now out the window. Not to mention this week's pay. "You don't have anything in the bank?" I ask.

Romy shoots me a dirty look. "We can't just walk in and open an account. Ten years ago humans didn't know we existed. We're supes. And now? Our rights are up in the air. This house is owned through a human proxy. Even now there's a law a bunch of Human Firsters are trying to push that says supes can't have assets. Some new asshole senator named Brent Anders. If that gets through, where will we be?"

I bite the inside of my cheek. The asshole in question is my ex. No need to share that with Canwella, though.

I stand. If there's one thing I know how to do, it's how to clean up a mess.

"Let's check on all the guests and get this place cleaned up," I say. "Maybe someone saw something. Also, I know a P.I. who can help. We'll find out who did this." I turn over the other chair and start picking up papers, putting them on Canwella's desk.

"We can't pay you," Romy says. "You might as well go home."

"You can pay me when we get back your money," I say, ignoring the way my stomach knots. But I can't do anything else. First of all, it's the way my dad taught me. You're loyal to your clients and hope they'll return the favor. But also, I like Canwella and when she can pay—I'll get that raise for sure.

Canwella nods. "Romy, do a room check. Make sure all the patrons are okay." She stands up. "Paige, come with me to the gaming hall. We'll see if anyone knows anything. Then we can get your P.I. friend involved if need be."

Customers are just starting to wake up when we get back to the room. There were five supes playing poker and a waiter who got zapped while mixing drinks. Canwella pours them each a tall glass of ambrosia and starts asking questions. I begin to tidy up the room but really I'm focused on them, listening for clues.

Unfortunately, no one seems to know anything. One person says there was only one guy, another says there were five. One says they were hit and stunned immediately, another says the masked man gave a little speech about the evils of gambling.

Romy joins us. "They stayed out of the rooms upstairs," she informs us. "No one up there even knew what was happening."

"Good, let's keep it that way." Canwella lowers her voice. "Do not tell anyone about the safe or all that missing money."

I nod. "When are all the"–I lower my voice–"bribes due?"

Canwella rubs her bulbous face. "The first of the month."

"But that's in a few days!"

"Mom, there's no way we can do that," Romy says. "Maybe we should shut it down."

Canwella turns on Romy and slaps her hard across the face. An ogre slap is no joke, and if Romy wasn't also an ogre she'd be flat on the floor with a broken jaw. Romy touches her face, her eyes shiny.

"Don't you ever say that again," Canwella tells her. "I built this place from the ground up. It's my life."

"I know," Romy spits. "You care about Charms more than you care about me!" She runs off.

Canwella looks at me. "I...my family life is complicated."

"Families always are," I tell her. I feel for them both. Canwella's business is about to go under, everything she built and loves. But Romy just wants her mom.

"Go home," Canwella tells me. "You look exhausted."

"Okay, but I'll come back tomorrow with my P.I. friend," I promise her. "Nico Tralano from Eye Wide Open Investigations."

"I know Nico. He's a good wolf." She lets out a deflated breath.

For a giant ogre, she looks so small and defeated. "I don't know what I am without Charms," she tells me. Surprisingly, I get that. Most people just see me as a cleaning lady, but running my business is a huge part of who I am.

"Hopefully, you won't have to find out," I tell her. She pulls out a bottle from behind the bar. "Here, take this. It's human scotch whiskey, very old. Drink it. Or sell it."

I hold up my hands. "I can't—" I start to say, but Canwella shoves it at me.

"Take it. You came through for me today. I appreciate that."

I nod and take the bottle, heading out to the Vanna. I ask her to drive me home so I can just sit and think.

Canwella and Romy don't deserve to have their lives destroyed.

I'm going to get their money back.

I'm going to save Charms.

5

When I get home I feel like I've walked into the wrong house.

My ex-husband Jax is there, for one, with his new girlfriend, Kimberly. She's a witch. And I don't mean that in an I-hate-her-for-dating-my-ex kind of way. She's a literal witch.

Nico is also there, holding Shit, who I forgot to pick up from doggie daycare. They must have called him when I failed to show up.

"What is going on?" I ask, searching for Darron. He struts toward me, wearing a beautiful vintage wool skirt suit that looks like it's something Marilyn Monroe would have worn.

"What is all this, Daphne?" I ask, using Darron's preferred name when she's dressed femme.

"It's an intervention, honey," she tells me. I look to the bottle of whiskey in my hands. "Not for you, for Shauna," she says, putting her hands on her padded hips.

"Oh. Right. Okay."

"Let's all make our way to the living room," Daphne announces. "There's tea and cookies."

Nico approaches me. He's holding Shit like a baby, rubbing his belly. Shit is loving every second of it. When the puppy sees me, though, he squirms out of Nico's arms and jumps into mine, licking my face. I nearly drop the bottle of whiskey but Nico saves it, looks at the label and says, "Nice."

"How did you get him?" I ask.

"You gave my information to the doggie daycare place?"

"Yeah. I wanted them to bill you for his care," I say, my chin high. "I figured it was part of the gift."

"They called me to get my credit card info. And said that I needed to replace a few other things too. Like all the toys he chewed through. And the door he managed to destroy. And the fence he broke apart. I paid for it all."

"Shit," I say, and the puppy, hearing his name, gives a little bark, then cuddles into my arms. "I can't pay you back," I tell him. "Charms might be closing down. I'm probably out of a job. I was going to ask you for help..." I peter off. It seems like I'm always asking Nico for help. "I can't pay you for that either."

He tilts his head, then holds up the bottle of whiskey. "If I can keep this, we'll call it even."

"Deal," I agree immediately.

"And you have to share a glass with me, one day."

I nod. "I'll fill you in after..." I motion around. "We're done with this."

"Okay. I know Canwella. She's a good egg."

Shit is laying his head on my shoulder and begins to snore softly.

"At least he's tired," Nico says. "I brought you a crate too. Might be worth it to try and crate train him."

"Thanks," I tell him. He's being so non-combative...it's

strange. And suddenly I'm in a weird moment. There's a warm puppy that this guy gifted me sleeping in my arms, he just invited me to have a drink with him, and now he's buying me stuff for my house. Our love/hate thing just got weirdly...domesticated.

"What the crap is this?" Shauna's voice echoes loudly from the next room. "Is this a party? Is this a party for me?" she asks. "Are those my cookies?"

"Honey, have a seat," Daphne's kind voice responds. "Have as many cookies as you want. We're here for you."

"Is it my birthday?" Shauna asks. "It's not. Wait...is this...?" Something clicks. "You dicks are NOT trying to intervention me!"

"We better get in there," I say to Nico as we go to face the wrath of Shauna.

Jax and Kimberly settle onto the couch, his arm tucked protectively around her shoulders. He must be serious about this girl, I realize. Even though there's a revolving door in Jax's love life, he rarely lets anyone in on his family life. If Kim's here to take a role in his sister's intervention, maybe Jax is finally settling down.

Speaking of settling down, Daphne has made herself comfortable in the only spare chair—which leaves the loveseat for me and Nico. Overstuffed cushions rest on each end of it, so we're pushed together, thighs touching. Shit makes a puppy grunt in his sleep, and slides out of my arms, stretching his body across both our laps.

"Tired, little man?" Nico asks, one hand rubbing up and down the pup's throat. He has large hands, strong and capable looking. Hands he can and no doubt has used to kill. But right now they are so soft and gentle as they stroke Shit. Shit makes a contented noise and I have to look away.

Ugh! This is the thing that always gets me about the bad

boys. The hard outer image versus the hidden softy gooey center. It's that dichotomy that keeps me coming back every time.

Of course, sometimes the soft gooey center isn't actually the center. It just hides the actual center at which sits a cheater. Like Jax. Or a total psycho. Like Brent. Or a fucking wolf. Like Nico.

The big question is—what's at Liam's center? He's not hard and tough on the outside. He's sweet and considerate. If this thing with his dad is just baggage from his past that he's carrying around—or more accurately, hiding in his dresser drawer—then I need to give this relationship my all.

No more giving Jax's new girlfriend the side-eye. No more enjoying the heat of Nico's thigh pressed against mine. No more wondering if Brent is happy with Giselle.

Those boys are like potato chips. Delicious, hard to resist, and very, very bad for me.

While Liam might just be what I've been looking for— what I need. A sweet potato fry of a man. Healthy but still scrumptious.

"Is it hot in here?" I ask no one in particular. Standing, I push Shit onto Nico's lap and then cross the room to crank one of the windows open. When that's done, I return to the loveseat, but instead of plopping back down next to Nico, I perch on the arm of the chair instead.

"Okay," Daphne says, tossing me a look that says "FOCUS." "Now that everyone's settled, let's get to business."

"This is bullshit," Shauna says, shoving cookies into her mouth, the crumbs falling down her chest and onto the carpet. "You jokers think you can judge me?" She pulls out her phone and starts fiddling with it.

"Shauna, dear," Daphne says, her high, warm voice

settling Shauna a little bit. "Please put your phone away and pay attention. We're not trying to judge you, but we need to talk about your issues."

"My issues?" she screeches, the moment of calm already over with. "What about *your* issues?" She throws her phone at Daphne. It bounces off a pillow and lands on the floor.

"I have plenty," Daphne tells her, crossing her arms and looking like the picture of calm, composure, and Doris Day. "But mine won't possibly put me in a permanent coma."

"This isn't about Daphne," I add.

"Jax does beauty too..." Shauna turns to her brother before Daphne can respond. "When he figured out he was fae and that he could use beauty as a drug...I had to watch his strung-out ass a buttload of times."

"That was years ago, Shauna," Jax says, taking Kimberly's hand. "Let's focus on now. Let's focus on you." I'm actually impressed with Jax not rising to the bait.

Shauna throws a cookie at him. "What? Suddenly you're all Mister Monogamy. How long is that gonna last? I mean, I like you, Kimmy, but it's not worth it to put a bunch of effort into your relationship. You'll be replaced in a month, tops."

"This is normal," Nico whispers to me. "She's lashing out."

"At least she hasn't..." I start, but then Shauna's eyes lock in on mine.

"And *you*..." Shauna reels on me. "You're worse than I am. Sex can be a drug too, Paige." I gulp, but she doesn't get a chance to continue. Shit has leapt from our laps and into Shauna's, teeth out, ruff raised. Except because he's part cat, it's not just his ruff that's on high alert. The Dalmanther's whole body is covered in raised hair, and he's doubled his size in less than a second.

"I don't think Shit is going to let you shit on Paige anymore," Nico says, a laugh in his voice.

"Alright," she says, swallowing hard in response to Shit's low growl. "But I'm not taking back anything I said," she adds, nose in the air.

"You don't have to," Jax says. "Because you're not wrong. I have been kind of a bastard to women in the past. In fact, Paige, I owe you an apology."

Oh, God. I put my hands up as Shit hops back onto the loveseat and puts his front paws on my legs. "This isn't your intervention, Jax," I tell him. "You don't have to ask for forgiveness. Let's not do this right now."

"Actually," Daphne says. "It's not a bad idea. While Shauna was trying to make you hurt," she raises an eyebrow at her, and Shauna has the grace to blush, "she's also not wrong. We're all going to say hard words to her here today. We have to be willing to hear some, ourselves."

She clears her throat, ready to share. "You're right, Shauna. I have my own issues, my own demons. When I lost my wife in the Great Ghosting it hit hard. It almost ruined me, just like losing Tina almost ruined you. She was the only person I thought I could ever love. But she's not the only one I've ever felt a connection to. I've just fought it off, fearful that forming a new relationship would be a breach, of sorts. I recognize that. After all, we don't know where anyone from the Ghosting went to, or if they could be back. But..."

Daphne's eyes soften as she weighs the decision. "I can't spend the rest of my life waiting for someone that might never show up. I'm making a vow here today to move on with my romantic relationships."

"That's not what I meant," Shauna says, a strangely horrified look on her face. "That's not what I meant at all."

There's some polite clapping and Shit raises his head, ears perked. When he decides there's no threat to me in the moment, he goes back to sleep.

"See Shauna, we're all learning from this experience." Jax says, giving Kim a squeeze. "I'm going to move on with my romantic life, too. And I'm starting with a clean slate." He takes a deep breath. "Paige, I was a terrible husband to you. I lied, I cheated, I messed everything up. You deserve way better than me, and I hope you find it."

"It's fine," I say, trying to keep it casual. But there are tears in my eyes. Shit lifts his head to lick them off my cheeks and I bury my face in his soft fur.

"How did this become about everyone's love lives?" Shauna asks. "This is supposed to be about me!" She collapses into a chair. "Well, are you bozos going to help me get straight or what?"

"Let's get to the point," I say, wiping my face. I'm glad Shauna seems eager to listen. "We're here because we love you, Shauna."

"I love you dorks too," Shauna says quietly.

"And we can't—won't—just stand by and watch you destroy yourself," Daphne adds.

"You don't understand," Shauna wails, throwing herself back against the chair. "My life has not been awesome. You know I was in jail, right? Underworld Reformatory. It was horrible. You have to wear collars that inhibit your supe powers, and—"

"My life hasn't been easy, either," I interrupt, temper rising. "My parents disappeared, my husband cheated on me, my business is failing, my ex-boyfriend tried to kill me." Shit lets out a little growl at my distress. "Grow up, Shauna. Just being sober isn't going to be enough to make Izzy let you into little KJ's life. She doesn't want another child to help her raise a child."

"That's a low blow, Paige Harper," Shauna says. She pops into her pixie form and screams at me. Flitting around the room she crashes into the table, knocking over the cookies and then buzzes past me.

I sigh.

I'm about done with Shauna's little pixie ass. And her giant pixie attitude.

6

I'm about to swat Shauna out of the air when she runs out of steam, lands on the table and collapses on her back, her tiny chest heaving.

"Are you done, dear?" Daphne asks, taking a sip of her tea.

"This isn't helpful, Shauna," Jax says.

"I don't think you even cared about Kit or Tina at all," I mutter.

Daphne gives me a look but surprisingly, Shauna snaps to attention. "What?!?"

I should have known going for the jugular was the best with Shauna.

I stand, hands on my hips. "Maybe you don't remember, because you blacked out right after Izzy told you this, but your brother, Kit, got killed because he was trying to figure out what happened to Tina. He was trying to solve the Ghosting and apparently some lead took him to O.H.I.O."

Shauna blinks at me. "I did sorta forget that. Or I thought I dreamed it. Izzy really, really, really said that?"

I nod. "She really, really did."

"Wait a minute." Nico grabs hold of my wrist, demanding attention. "Why is this the first I'm hearing of this?"

Shaking him loose, I shrug. "I don't have to tell you everything." I don't add that I probably would've told him just to get his take on it, but that so much else has been going on it didn't cross my mind.

"Paige," Jax stands too. "You didn't tell me either. And I have an O.H.I.O. connection!"

"They framed you for murder, Jax!" I remind him, not hiding my exasperation. "That's not a helpful connection."

"I think we're getting sidetracked," Kimmy says softly.

"Agreed," Daphne quickly adds.

"I've got a client to see," Nico announces, standing abruptly.

"You mean to fuck," I mutter. It's not meant to reach Nico's ears, but I forget that his wolf side makes his hearing extra keen.

Turning to me, he grabs hold of my chin and leans in so close our lips almost touch. "Jealous?"

"No!"

"Then what do you care?" He smiles just slightly and then releases me. Turning on his heel, he adds as he exits the room, "If you figure out the identity of VSK I'd appreciate a phone call or at least a text."

I roll my eyes at Nico acting butt hurt because I didn't tell him some small bit of news. Collapsing into the loveseat, I pull Shit on top of me.

Shauna meanwhile has been unusually quiet. Finally she says, "I can't kill Brent because he's our only connection to O.H.I.O. If they really are behind the Ghosting..." She goes quiet again, only her jaw working as she chews on cookies, shoving in one after another.

"Yesterday I didn't think we were even going to be able to wake you up," Daphne says quietly. "You've got to stop hitting the beauty, or one day you won't. And then who will go after Brent and O.H.I.O.? Who will avenge Kit's death?"

Shauna doesn't say anything, just crosses her arms with a thoughtful expression.

"Look, sis," Jax says, "I know how awesome beauty feels. And that's part of the reason I was such a philanderer. But I can tell you that having a real, solid, emotionally checked-in relationship is way better than any beauty hit."

Kim smiles and rests her head on his shoulder, reaching for his hand.

"I get what you're saying," Shauna says. "I gotta find out what happened to Tina and get her back. And I guess those other people who ghosted too. But mostly Tina."

I trade looks with Daphne. I don't know if sending Shauna on some wild goose chase to bring back Tina is the way to get her to quit beauty. As much as I hate to admit it, it seems hopeless. Who knows if Kit was even right about O.H.I.O. having a hand in the Ghosting?

Daphne gives a little shrug and then says, "We'll help you in any way we can, Shauna."

"Of course you will," Shauna says, already snapping back to her normal self-centered self. "And we'll be heroes. Like way better than when I worked at the FBI..."

Wait, whut? My head snaps to Jax and he gives me a nod.

How did I not know that Shauna worked for the FBI? How is that even possible? Now is definitely not the time to ask; she's on a roll of self-discovery.

"I quit the FBI after Tina disappeared. I stopped seeing all my friends; it was too hard. They looked at me like I was missing something, and I was...Tina. Then my family kicked me out of Faerieland for being such a downer. And yes, I hit the beauty. Hard. Love like Tina and I had only comes along once in a lifetime."

"But you could have another type of love," I tell her, trying to make her entire recovery not hinge on finding Tina. "Little KJ needs you. You're his aunt, and his mom said you can be in his life if you can be a positive influence. But coming home trashed from some beauty pageant and carrying two boxes of donuts isn't a positive influence."

"I know, I know," she admits, wiping her face. "And you're right. I do need to do it for KJ. He needs two aunts. Both me and Tina. Two positive role models. I gotta get clean and get her back. It's just...it's so hard."

"That's why we're here to help," Daphne says, coming over to Shauna and putting her hand on her knee. "You don't have to do this alone. We're all here because we have your back. And look, I've got a picture here of KJ," she whips out her phone and shows Shauna. "Every time you feel like you need a hit of beauty, look at this instead. This is real beauty. The kind that doesn't fade."

"Or put you into a magically-induced coma," Kim adds as Jax pats her hand.

Shauna nods, touching the screen. "Can you send this to me?"

"Of course," Daphne says.

"You can look at it whenever you need extra motivation," I say.

"Whatever," Shauna says. "I just want it so when Tina gets back she can get caught up on little KJ and what she missed."

"Right," I nod, realizing that Shauna is determined to run with this 'find Tina' thing. "Or that."

"I'm going to do it!" Shauna jumps to her feet. "I'm going

cold turkey on the beauty…and no more sugar!" She sweeps the cookies off the table.

"Wait a second…" I start. Leave it to Shauna to make this harder than it already is.

"Sugar is my gateway drug," she insists. "I'm off it. Starting now!"

I exchange a glance with Daphne. "Is that such a good idea?"

"There's the Whole Ass Diet," Kim pipes up, and everyone looks at her. "No really," she says. "The founder said if you're going on a diet you can't half-ass it. So it's the Whole Ass Diet. No sugar for 30 days. None. No sweeteners, no fruit, and definitely no donuts."

Shauna's eyes have glazed over at the thought. "I can do it…" she says softly.

"You can if we help," I say. "I won't bring anymore junk food home, and we'll clean out the cupboards tonight, get rid of everything with sugar. That way you won't be tempted."

Shauna brightens a little. "Can we eat it in order to get rid of it?"

"I don't think it works that way," Daphne says gently.

"And if you leave the house, take Shit with you," I say, warming up to my idea. "He's incredibly smart, and I bet we can teach him to detect sugar, and warn you if you're about to eat any. Would that work?"

"You'll probably need more blood," Kim hazards. "I think your fae aspect, the sugar, the beauty binges, have suppressed a bit of your vamp side. You need to keep your-self fed."

"Where are we going to get blood?" I ask. I know there are delivery services now that cater to vamps. But those are expensive.

"I can get you some," Kim says. She's a witch so she has connections. "Let me make a few calls."

"This could work…" I say, actually believing it. Well, fifty percent believing it, but faking like I think it's a sure thing.

"I'm going to try," Shauna says, squeezing her eyes shut. "No, I'm going to *do* it."

"That's my girl," Daphne says, patting her knee. "I have to change and get to work, but I'm only a phone call away if you need me," she tells Shauna."

"And I've got to run too. I've got a cow abscess to drain," Kim says, standing up.

"But I'm going to stay with you here tonight," Jax assures her. "It's going to be a rough ride and we'll all chip in time. We want you to succeed, Shauna."

I'm amazed at how far Jax has come. "I don't have anything half as exciting as a cow abscess," I say, rising as well.

Daphne approaches me. "I can take tomorrow during the day with Shauna but I need you back here in the evening. I have a play rehearsal I can't miss."

"I can totally do that," I assure her.

Jax makes his way toward me. My handsome fae ex-husband. I want to simultaneously hug him and hit him. "I hope it's okay I'm here. I just wanted to help out…" he starts.

"It's fine," I tell him. "How did you get in, anyway?" Jax and I made a bargain a while back that he would never "darken my doorstep." Unfortunately, fae are tricksters and he only literally meant he wouldn't cross through the doorway.

"Well, since you locked up the widow's walk entrance I had to fly in through the window. You know, we can make a new deal where I'm allowed to come in the door…"

"Nope. Not happening," I tell him. But I'm mostly just

joking with him. My anger toward Jax and all the shitty stuff he did to me when we were together is finally starting to fade.

I walk Kimmy to the door, only to find Nico waiting on my porch.

"I remembered you wanted to talk with me after," he says shortly.

I can tell he's still pissed, but at the same time, he was good enough to stick around—just because he said that he would. That's the kind of dependability a girl—

I cut that thought off. Not going there, I remind myself. "Thanks," I tell Nico as Shit squeezes past my legs and runs to the corner of the house to take a piss all over my hydrangea bush.

"There was a stick-up at Charms," I tell Nico.

"Isn't that the whole idea?" he asks, and I shove his shoulder.

"No, I mean they got robbed," I tell him. "I was there. A guy took a shot at me, but luckily he only had a supe stun gun."

Nico's smile is instantly wiped away. "Are you okay?"

"Yeah, I'm fine. It's just that if Canwella can't recoup her money, I'm out my pay and given how things are going, my business is sunk. And she was just so upset..."

"A crying ogre is not pretty," Nico muses, then opens the door and whistles at Shit, who obediently goes inside, giving my hand a push with his nose as he passes me.

"I was thinking we could go check it out in the morning," I say, with a hopeful smile. "Once Canwella gets her money back, I know she can pay you."

Nico frowns. "But I thought that I only take on clients I also want to screw."

"Okay, I'm sorry. I shouldn't have said that," I admit. "Forgive me?"

"Of course." Nico gives me one of his wolfish grins. "I deal with jealous ladies all the time. I know how you get when you want something you can't have."

I punch him in the arm. And then have to shake out my hand. Ouch. "You're so full of yourself," I tell him. "And for the record. I could have you right now, on this porch if I wanted to."

"Oh yeah?" Nico leans in closer, his breath warm on my cheek. "Even with him standing right there?"

"Paige?"

I whirl around to find Liam on my doorstep with a bouquet of flowers and a bottle of wine. My heart leaps in my chest, my pulse picks up, and I want to throw himself into his arms...until I remember that I've never told him where I live.

7

Niko squares off and sniffs at Liam. Shit tears through the screen door, leaving a hole in his wake. Luckily, Nico snatches his collar and holds him tight so that Liam doesn't end up with a similar hole.

"How…" I shake my head, backing away. A lot of traumatic shit has gone down on my porch lately and I'm not ready for anything else right now. "What are you doing here?"

My tone must not be the most welcoming, because Liam flinches. There's another little hop in my pulse, but this one feels like a warning. *Don't forget about the picture*, my body seems to be telling me. *Don't forget he could be a killer.*

"I hate how we left things this morning," he says, glancing at Nico. "Hello there…large and looming person."

Nico doesn't move. He does glower, though.

"This is Nico…a friend. He has the office next to mine. He's a werewolf," I add for no good reason.

"Oh, that's interesting. My friends would love to meet a real live werewolf, maybe you can come to game night one time…"

"I don't play games," Nico growls.

Oh, good lord. Not only do I have to worry that my maybe-boyfriend is a maybe-killer, but I also have to protect him from Nico, just in case he's not.

"Liam, why are you here?" I ask.

He shakes his head. "Oh, right. I know you had to run"–he lowers his voice–"this morning, so I thought I'd bring you flowers to let you know that I'm thinking of you."

Once again, my heart feels warm but my mind is shouting—*red flag, red flag!*

"But how do you know where I live?" I ask.

"Not cool, man," Nico growls. "And really suspicious."

Liam looks beyond confused. "I...was invited, though." He pulls out his phone. "Oh bugger. Did I get the wrong end of the stick?" He starts to read. "'S'up, English dude. Shauna here. My friends are having a party to celebrate my awesomeness. Stop by. Paige needs some D.' And she gave me the address..." he trails off and blushes. "I mean, I didn't come because of that last part but..." He awkwardly thrusts the flowers at me. "I am so sorry if"–he glances again at Nico–"if I'm not welcome."

"No!" I stop him, relief flooding me. "I'm glad to see you, truly. I was just confused."

"It wasn't a party," Nico tells him. "It was an intervention."

"Oh...then...this is probably not appropriate," he says, brandishing the bottle of wine.

"It's not that kind of intervention," I explain. "I showed up with a bottle of whiskey, actually."

Liam smiles at me although it wobbles and then falls as his gaze turns to Shit, who is still growling at him.

"Is that a Dalmanther?" he asks.

"This is Shit," I say. Liam looks like he's about to ask

about the name, so I quickly add, "Long story, I'll tell you later." To Shit I add, "Be nice."

Darron comes bursting through the door dressed in his work clothes, red swim trunks and a lifeguard shirt. He sports a duffel bag with the name of the retirement community–Eternity–embroidered on the side. He manages to even make this basic ensemble look fashionable. "What is this...?" he asks, his eyes pinging from Liam to Nico and back again.

"Nothing. Aren't you late for work?" I ask.

"Oh, honey, for drama like this? I'll make time." He puts down his duffel bag and crosses his arms. Then Shauna bursts out of the house, Jax on her heels.

"Liam, you came!" she shouts.

"I did, yes," he says. Even in the evening light, I can see his face burn bright red.

"Guess what? I'm going to get clean!"

"That's great," he tells her. "Really, Shauna. Congrats."

"I'm going to get drunk to celebrate!" she declares.

"Oh, sis, you need to know that alcohol is basically sugar," Jax says, taking her by the shoulders and leading her back inside.

"That can't be true," she says.

"I'm afraid it is," he tells her.

"Oh, fart. All the best things have sugar." She crosses her arms over her chest. "I think I'm going into withdrawal."

"You had a cookie ten minutes ago," I remind her. I turn to Darron who is practically drooling over the thought of a Nico/Liam throwdown.

"You, go to work," I order.

"Fine," he tells me, picking up his bag and heading down the path to the street. "But you'd better tell me everything that happens," he shouts over his shoulder, spinning on his heel.

"We could go inside and open that bottle of wine," I offer Liam.

"That wouldn't be fair to Shauna...so wait, is she giving up sugar? Is that what this intervention is about?"

"No, beauty...you know how fae use it as a drug? Well, she got it into her head that she needed to stop sugar as well."

"Good for her," Liam says. "I hope it works."

What was I thinking? Liam is so nice. He is definitely not VSK. And if he is, it's better I play along, right?

"Maybe we could go out to a pub?" Liam says. "You can come too," he glances at Nico.

"We can't," Nico pushes forward. "We have that case at Charms."

"I thought we were waiting until the morning..." I start.

"No time like the present," he tells me, taking my elbow and ushering me off the porch. "Sorry old chap, maybe next time," he says to Liam.

"Okay then," Liam says. "I'll call you!" he shouts at my retreating form.

I shake Nico off when we reach his car. "What the hell was that all about?"

"Work," Nico returns.

"Suuure. That was one hundred percent totally all about work."

"Well, I am a professional," he says, his one eye gleaming mischievously.

"A professional dick," I shoot back.

"I'm not denying it." He opens the passenger side door for me, and leans in. He smells amazing. It's almost like a drug.

But if Shauna can stop using beauty and sugar then surely I can stop with the bad boys. I look back at Liam. He waves cheerfully. He doesn't even look suspicious or jealous that I'm leaving with an extremely hot one-eyed werewolf.

There's something so inherently sweet and good in him. I think. I hope.

"Hold on," I say to Nico and then I run back to Liam, throw my arms around his neck, and kiss him.

"Oh!" he says, clearly taken by surprise. But it doesn't take him long to adjust.

Whatever else he is, Liam definitely knows how to kiss a girl. His hands come around my back, pulling me closer and I let myself melt into him.

Maybe Shauna is right. I do need some D.

Nico leans on the horn.

"Paige," Liam pants. "I don't want to keep you, but I also really do want to keep you."

"Let's do dinner tomorrow," I say. Part of me is offering because I want to get him out of his apartment so that McGinnis can snoop around and clarify once and for all that this guy is exactly what I think he is—a good catch. But I can't deny that another part of me—a large part—really wants to see him again.

Liam grimaces. "I've got a tour tomorrow. Could you do the day after?"

"It's a date," I say and then press one more kiss to his cheek.

"I'm putting you on my schedule, Paige Harper," he calls after me as I practically skip back toward Nico's car.

"On my shed-jewel too," I yell back, trying to mimic his adorable accent. Pulling the car door open, I collapse into the seat beside Nico.

He looks at me with a dangerous gleam in his eye. "A kiss with your boyfriend, but a trip to the brothel with me."

Before I can respond, he throws the car into reverse and tires squeal as we take off down the driveway and into the night.

8

At Charms, Romy is playing bartender, but mostly it looks like she's serving herself. The downstairs parlor is empty. Word must have gotten out about the robbery and people don't feel safe playing poker here.

"Hey Paige, you here to watch it all burn?" Romy pours herself a generous glass of ambrosia, then lights up a cigarette and takes a long drag. I quit smoking years ago but every once in a while I indulge. And it's been that kind of day.

"Can I snag one of those?" I ask.

She tosses me the pack and a match book. I almost drop the matches when I see the name on it. Monkey Business Motel. Ugh. It's a low-key no-tell-motel off the highway. After I caught Jax cheating on me—literally catching him in the act—I started digging to find out if it was "just this one time" like he swore it was. Of course, it wasn't just the one time. His glove box was full of wadded up receipts from the Monkey Business Motel. When I shoved them in his face, he told me they were from business meetings. "Business is right there in the name." That's when I kneed him in the balls, unable to stand anymore lies.

"Canwella around?" Nico asks, breaking into my unhappy flashback.

"Yeah, she's in her office. She's trying to call in some favors."

"How's that going?" I ask.

"Not great." Romy says, shaking her head.

I light up the cigarette and take a few puffs. Damn, it tastes good. "Can you tell her I'm here with my P.I. friend?"

"Sure thing." She gulps down her drink. "Help yourself to whatever booze you want."

I lean over and grab a glass and a bottle of vodka. Why not? It's been a long day.

Nico and I sit at the bar and wait for Canwella and I fiddle with the matchbook. It occurs to me that there's another way that I can put my doubts about Liam to rest.

"Remember when Giselle was dumped at my house and you said you got VSK's scent?" I ask Nico.

"I'm not going to forget that, am I?" Nico says. He grabs himself a beer and chugs it down, then grabs another one. He makes a show of leaving a twenty on the bar though.

I shrug. If I'm not going to get paid, I can at least drink my weight in vodka.

"So, if you came in contact with him again, you'd know it?"

"Likely, yes."

I raise an eyebrow. "Likely?"

"Look, it's not an exact science. Smell can be faked or hidden, sure. It can even be magically changed. VSK is smart. I know nothing about him. He could just be some human with a vendetta, or he could be some magical user. There's no way to be one hundred percent."

"But…" I say, "If VSK was just a human who didn't hide their scent, you'd be able to sniff them out? If you came in contact with them, you'd recognize them immediately."

"Yes." He tilts his head at me.

"And that hasn't happened…" I lead.

"Do you think I'd keep that from you?" he asks. "What are you getting at?"

"Nothing!" I say, gulping down my vodka and taking one last drag on my cigarette before smashing it out. "I just want to make sure I know how it works."

I shrug like it doesn't matter, but my heart is giving these painful little hopeful leaps. Nico stood right next to Liam and didn't smell VSK. Maybe those pictures were just Liam's way of handling his daddy issues. If that's his only hang-up, I can deal with that. It still makes him a bazillion times less screwed up than anyone else I've ever been with.

Romy reappears. "Mom will see you in her office now," she tells me.

I leave the pack of cigarettes behind, pushing the Monkey Business Motel matchbook into the crinkly plastic. I don't need the temptation of smoking the rest of the pack. Nico rises first and gives me a grand, sweeping gesture, indicating for me to go in front of him. I return the movement, with an eyebrow raised. "Don't you know it's dangerous to turn your back on a wild animal?"

"Only if you don't trust them," Nico shoots back.

We're going to be stuck in a showdown of both of us half bowing and telling the other one to go first if I don't end this soon. I think of Liam on the porch, both his smile and the flowers seeming to wilt when he spotted Nico.

"Well, I don't," I say sternly. He huffs and walks in front of me, making a big show of holding the office door open. I brush past him, ignoring how good he smells, or how I can feel the heat radiating off of him. I know cats have a higher resting body temperature than people, but do dogs? Or more specifically, werewolves?

My thoughts are interrupted when Canwella rises from behind her desk. It's like watching a hill move through a house. Except this hill has eyes—with matching streams of water running from them.

"I'm so sorry," Nico says, moving around her desk easily and wrapping an arm around her massive shoulders. He has to stand on tiptoe to do it, and I revel a little in the fact that not every woman of every species is rattled by him.

"Thanks," Canwella says, wiping her nose on his arm and leaving behind a visible trail. "I just don't know what we're going to do."

"We're going to find out who did this to you, and make them pay," Nico says, politely ignoring his dripping sleeve as he takes a seat. "Let's start with who might want to hurt your business."

"That's a longer list than you might think," Canwella says with a sniff as I take the seat next to Nico's. "Not everyone is supportive of turning the act of love into a commodity."

"Anyone specifically, though?" I press. I know I've had more than my share of problems—and threats—from humans ever since I very publicly saved Shauna from being attacked in a park. "How about Humans First? Any problems with them?"

"Ha!" Canwella says with a smirk. "My only issue with them is that they want to be first in line. Bunch of hypocrites."

"What?" I ask, genuinely surprised. "You have Firsters as customers?"

"Oh, honey, they're half my clientele."

I grimace, wondering if I've ever cleaned up any mess left behind by Brent in the rooms upstairs. I mean, I can't claim to have Nico's nose, so it's totally possible.

"We should focus on other supes, I think," Nico interjects. "Paige, you said the guy who took a shot at you had a stun gun?"

"Yes," I say, nodding. "He came armed for supes, not humans. But that doesn't mean he wasn't human, right? He might have just assumed since it's a supe establishment—"

"Did he seem to know his way around?" Nico asks, running over my words.

"As a matter of fact, *canine interruptus*, I didn't see him actually rob anything. I interrupted him, threatened him with my gun, and he ran." I snap. "Like a little bitch."

Canwella barks out a laugh that turns into a choking sneeze, and more tears run down her face before she can speak again. "Nico is right. It might seem crazy, but I've got more supe enemies than human ones."

"Enemies?" I jump right on that. "Who could hate you?"

It's true. Canwella might not be attractive to look at, but inside is a heart of gold. Not to mention the voice of an opera star.

"My first instinct is it's those bastards over at The Monarch Club."

"Are you still butting heads with those boys?" Nico asks. He looks my way to clue me in. "The Monarchs are a low-level crime family. They tried to buy out Canwella a few years ago."

"If by 'buy out' you mean strongarm me into paying them 'protection' money, then yes, that's pretty much what happened. We've been fighting with them ever since. I hate them," she spits. "Jimmy Monarch is a dirtbag. If he was on fire I wouldn't offer to piss on him."

"They'll be top on our list," Nico says, decisively, not even bothering to confer with me first. I mean, it's the right call, but geez, he could at least let me give a nod of assent. "Anything else, anything weird leading up to today...?"

"No, everything was fine," Canwella says.

"Wait," I interject. "Seraphina was out today."

"Oh, that's right, with all the excitement I totally forgot." Canwella frowns. "It's hard to imagine her as a suspect. The poor girl has always been so delicate. She barely leaves her room. I have all her meals brought to her."

"Yeah, but you gotta admit the timing is suspicious. Is she still gone?" I ask.

Canwella calls Romy in to go check. "She's been real big into that Together To Come podcast. The girls and guys upstairs started listening to it for a laugh. The host says humans and supes must come together or destroy each other."

"Ohhh..." My eyes go wide. "I've heard of this guy; when he says come together, he means it literally. He wants us to bang out our differences."

"Doesn't seem like a terrible theory to me," Nico says. He leans into my space, his breath warm on my cheek. "What do you think, Paige? Make love not war?"

I shove him away, not liking the way his words in that rough voice of his shoot right to my groin. "Why are those always the only two options? How about make soup not war? Or make socks not war? We'll all take up knitting and our hands will be too busy for fighting and our feet will be toasty and warm."

Canwella gives a low sultry chuckle. "That would put me out of business; not that I'm afraid of that. No way most humans are gonna want to knit instead of fuck."

"No, ma'am," Nico heartily agrees. Again he looks my

way and this time I can't repress a shiver. His one uncovered eye is sleepy and hooded when it locks onto mine. "Paige, if you need a reminder as to why sex is better than crafting, I'll volunteer my time to help you compare and contrast the two activities."

"I bet you don't even know how to knit," I shoot back and am disgusted that I sound slightly breathless.

Closing the distance between us, Nico's hands cover mine. With my hands inside his much larger ones he mimes as if we are holding knitting needles. "My mother taught me, actually. We lived hand to mouth growing up, so she'd make us gloves, hats, and even socks." His face is soft for a moment, as if remembering better times, but then he grimaces. "Unfortunately for your world peace theory, I saw her more than once use those same knitting needles to stab an enemy through the ear...or sometimes the eye."

Abruptly he drops my hands and steps away, shoving his hands in his pockets. I take a half step toward him, wanting to comfort him, because it's obvious that memory churned up something dark and painful inside him. But I pull back, reminding myself that Nico is a big werewolf and can take care of himself.

Canwella lets out a little laugh. "My oh my, that was interesting."

I go red, because for a few minutes there I honestly forget Canwella was even in the room. I hate that Nico can get into my head like that. No, not my head. It's definitely a lower part of my body that he's affecting.

9

Thankfully I'm saved by Romy poking her head into the room

"Seraphina is still gone," she says.

"Shit, what did that girl get into? Tell me as soon as she gets back," Canwella orders Romy. With an impatient wave, she sends Romy away. "Close the door behind you.".

"Anyone else stand out to you right now?" I ask.

"How about a rival business owner?" Canwella asks, and Nico perks up.

"Super Au Naturale?" Nico asks, but the tone isn't a question. It's a statement.

"Yeah," Canwella nods, then turns to me. "They're a lowbrow joint on the other side of town," she explains. "All nude, all the time, super raunchy."

"Umm..." I don't know what to say to that. Canwella keeps things pretty classy, as far as a whorehouse is concerned, but even I have blushed once or twice while cleaning up the *Three's Company* room.

"No, hon," Canwella says. "We're talking unsafe working conditions. I vet my customers and consistently check the health of my workers. Plus I take pride in making sure my guys and girls upstairs want to be here. Nobody does anything they don't want to do. But at Au Naturale anybody can walk in and ask for anything—and they'll get it. No questions asked."

"Up to and including violence," Nico says, a muscle in his jaw twitching. "I helped a family get their fae daughter out of a contract there after a guy beat her for kicks."

"Oh…" I say. "I was wondering how you knew about its existence." He raises an eyebrow at me and I glance away, unable to stop a blush from rising in my cheeks.

"I don't have to pay for it," he reminds me.

"No, they pay you," I shoot back.

"Do I need to put you two in the foreplay room?" Canwella asks.

"I have a boyfriend," I say, a little too stiffly. "He's British," I add.

"There's the *Prince Albert* room," Canwella says, ignoring the comment about my boyfriend. I'd push it…except for the fact that technically Liam isn't my boyfriend. She leers at Nico. "If that's the kind of thing you like!"

He grins sheepishly, "I have to admit I don't know what that is," he says. "I don't always get human references…" he shrugs.

"Google it later," I tell him and pointedly face Canwella. "Let's focus on you," I push forward. "Why would Au Naturale come after Charms?"

"I've got a mole on their staff," Canwella admits. "An ogre bouncer. Whenever any of their girls or guys are being maltreated, he lets them know to come here for work instead. And last month…"

She takes a deep breath, shoots a glance at Nico.

"Last week he told me they had an underage minotaur

in there. Special clients only. Top dollar. I reported it to the human authorities, but…"

Nico snorts. "I'm sure that went nowhere."

"They weren't interested," Canwella confirms. "So I may have taken matters into my own hands. She's back with her family now, and safe as can be expected. But I'm sure they knew it was me behind it. We've had our tangles in the past, and who else would care?"

"That sounds about right," Nico agrees. "Harmargan wouldn't think twice about striking back at you. In fact, it sounds like you got off easy."

"Har…mar…gan?" I ask, sounding out the syllables awkwardly.

"The cyclops that runs Au Naturale," he explains. "He's old as dirt and mean as hell. You'll see when we meet him."

"And we're doing this when exactly?"

"Don't worry," Nico says easily. "It won't interfere with your date."

"How about *why* am I even going with you?" I bristle.

"I agree with Paige," Canwella says. "This is not a good idea."

"Thank you," I say, settling back into my chair.

"It's too risky for you to be seen in there, Nico," Canwella goes on.

"Wait—what?" I shoot forward. "You're worried about *him*?"

"Harmargan knows Nico," Canwella says. "He'll have a target on his back the moment he walks in. But he doesn't know you, Paige. You can go in, free and clear with no suspicion."

"Great," I mutter. "Send the human into the seedy supe establishment."

"But not by yourself," Nico warns. "That's not happening."

"The front rooms are more on the up and up," Canwella explains. "You've got to work your way into the back and down to the basement for the special services."

"Do you know anyone who would go with you?" Nico asks. "And I'm not trying to be a shit when I say not the Brit. He couldn't protect you from a gust of wind."

"The best way to get into the basement would be if you could pose as a seller," Canwella suggests.

"A seller?" I wince. "Please tell me you mean a seller of lube and condoms."

"Pretty sure she's talking about supe trafficking," Nico says. "And that's actually genius. Bring in a supe who looks like a victim, but can actually be back up if you need it."

I frown at Nico, knowing exactly who he's talking about. "You want me to bring strung-out Shauna? Seriously?"

He shrugs. "Might be good for her. Seems like with her whole 'save Tina' thing that she needs goals to work towards in order to stay on the right track. The Tina thing is gonna be a..." He pauses, not saying impossible, but definitely thinking it. Finally he settles on, "A long haul type situation. Might be nice for her to score a few little wins before she gets there. Plus she used to do stuff like this all the time. She worked for the FBI, remember."

"That's a great point," I say, and I mean it. But also I see an opportunity to help Shauna and make Nico's life a little more difficult. "Why not bring her on as an assistant?"

"Woah. Hold up," Nico says, actually holding his hands up as if to fend off an imaginary Shauna. "You are not roping me into babysitting Shauna."

"Oh c'mon, you said yourself Shauna used to work for the FBI," I point out and then can't help but add, "I'm so grateful to you for giving me Shit that I want to give you a little shit too."

Nico groans and shakes his head. "Okay, how about this...you bring Shauna with you tomorrow and if it goes well...I'll think about it."

"Less thinking, more doing," I counter, holding out a hand so we can shake on it.

Nico gives me a wolfish smile. "And you want me to do Shauna?"

"No!" I snap, surprised by the little frisson of jealousy that snakes through at the thought of Nico and Shauna hooking up. Not that she'd ever be interested. Shauna wants Tina or nothing. Still... "Work with her, don't—" I wave a hand, deciding it's beneath my dignity to finish that sentence.

Unfortunately, I forget that we're having this conversation in the whorehouse. With the owner.

"Don't bang her," Canwella says in her beautiful voice. And then either to drive the point home or maybe to just show off her knowledge, she adds, "And that means no fadoodling or playing nug a nug either. I think she'd also prefer you refrain from dancing the kipples, joining giblets, or any horizontal refreshment."

Nico's eye glints at me with humor. "Don't worry, Paige. I'll take good care of Shauna—"

"In bed," Canwella says with a bawdy laugh, at the same time that Nico finishes with, "If we end up working together."

I've dropped the hand I held out for a handshake, but Nico picks it up and seals his palm to mine. "And you'll owe me one," he says, using my hand to pull me closer. "You'll owe me big," he repeats his voice low and rough and sending sparks through my body.

I jerk away, taking my hand with me. It almost burns from his touch. Like I've been playing with fire. Which is not a smart thing to do, I remind myself, not matter how much my body screams for me to press my bare skin against Nico's.

"Wow," Canwella remarks, her gaze flitting between the two of us. "The two of you just need to clunge plunge and get it out of your system."

"It'll happen," Nico says at the exact same time I reply, "Never gonna happen."

Canwella laughs her amazing tinkling laugh, while I stare at Nico and wonder which one of us will end up eating our words.

10

———

The next day I go to the office hoping to scare up some more clients. There's a message on my answering machine from an older lady I've done work for before. She's a hoarder and screams at me not to move anything while at the same time wanting me to get rid of the dirt and dust surrounding all her piles of crap. I dread working for her, but she always pays, and I need the money.

I return the client's call and set up a time to clean for her later in the week.

Next door I hear the low rumble of Nico's voice as he talks on the phone.

Okay, I mentally amend, I'm attracted to one very specific shifter. But that, I remind myself for the millionth time, is never gonna happen.

There's depressingly little to do after that except feed Vee and then shuffle around some unpaid bills trying to decide which ones I can let go past their due dates and which ones I need to cough up for.

Finally, Nico pokes his head in.

"We're still on for tonight?" I ask. "We were going to

check out the Monarch Club first, then maybe hit up Au Naturale if Canwella can get us in touch with her mole there.

"Oh, no." he shrugs. "That's what I came to tell you. I went last night. They're clear."

I blink hard. "You went last night?"

"After I dropped you off at home." He smiles tightly.

"I thought we were going together," I say.

"Why would I need you for that?" He tilts his head. "You're not my partner, Paige."

That hurts more than it should. "I'm not, but I did get you this job. We're in it together."

"We're not. Not really. My business isn't Eye Wide Open Plus Paige Investigations." He leans against the doorframe looking like a Gap model. Anger simmers in my belly.

I take a deep breath. "And with your amazing investigation skills you discovered that...?"

"The Monarchs were robbed too. It must have been a crew that hit a bunch of supe businesses. They're not behind it."

"Well great. I guess you don't need me anymore," I say. I stand and walk toward him, and I must look pissed because he backs up. I shut the door in his face. Then I lock it. And for good measure I close the blinds.

Nico Tralano can go stick a dick in his private eye.

It's not a great morning.

When I get home in time to relieve Darron of his duties, he looks frazzled.

Shauna, surprisingly, looks happy as a baby. She's curled on the couch with a celebrity magazine (Headline: IS OPRAH SECRETLY A SUPE!?!) and a giant bulge of something tucked into her cheek that she sucks on contentedly.

"Hi?" I say as I try to feel out the mood of the room.

Shauna grins up at me and a line of candy-colored drool drips from the corner of her mouth. "Hewo, Paige. Dawon gave me a sugar-free jawbreaker and it's dewicious."

I look at Darron with raised eyebrows. I get a death glare in response, even as he responds in a cheerful voice, "Yes I did, and I'm so glad you're enjoying it."

"Dis sugar fwee thing isn't so hard," Shauna says. "You just gotta find the fings you like." Her eyes light up. "Speaking of..." She spits the jawbreaker into the palm of her hand so she can speak more clearly. It's gigantic, the size of a golf ball. "Could you please make me more of that green tea? It tastes so yummy."

"Of course, darling," Darron says. His hand closes in a death grip around my arm. "I'll show Paige just how I do it so she can make it for you too when I'm at rehearsal."

Popping the jawbreaker back into her mouth, Shauna happily hums her assent and goes back to her magazine while Darron hustles me into the kitchen.

Once there, he releases me as he goes to put the kettle on. Then he collapses into a chair.

I take the chair beside him. "Darron, are you okay?"

"She broke me," he admits in a low voice. He looks at me and there's a sort of horror in his eyes. "I've seen things in my years. Horrible things. But this..." He scrubs both hands over his face. "Every minute that she went without sugar, she became less and less stable. I went into the bathroom, just to have a moment to compose myself and she busted through the door. Shredded it into tiny little toothpicks." His eyes go dark. "You know how they say an approaching tornado sounds like a train? That's what she was. I could see the destruction gathering around her. I was afraid she'd take down the house—maybe even the whole neighborhood.

Even Shit is exhausted. He hid upstairs and passed out on your bed."

"My god," I say, believing him completely. Shauna on her best days can be destructive. But at her worst? I can easily imagine her having the force of an atomic bomb.

"I offered to make her some green tea to calm her down," Darron continues as the kettle starts to whistle. He pours the kettle into a nearby mug with a tea bag waiting inside of it. Then he pulls the sugar bowl from the cupboard. "I put just a little sugar in," he says, keeping his voice low so Shauna doesn't overhear. "Just to take the edge off." I watch as he puts in three giant heaping spoonfuls of sugar. For me it's a lot of sugar, but for Shauna...it's almost nothing. She usually likes enough sugar in her beverages that you can hear it crunch between her teeth.

He puts the mug into my hands. "The tea helped but she was still not in a good place and I was so done. I just needed a break. That's when I gave her the jawbreaker."

"It's not actually sugar-free, is it?" I ask.

Darron gives me a 'are you an idiot' look. "No, it's not," he confirms. "Look, sugar isn't her problem. It's the beauty. But thinking she can kick sugar will give her the confidence to work through her beauty addiction. Let's just help her along." He makes a pushing motion.

"It's okay," I put a hand on Darron's shoulder. "I would've done the same thing and I probably would've broken way sooner."

"Thanks." He gives me a grateful smile. "I'm going to leave for rehearsal a little bit early, just so I can have some time to gather myself."

"Of course," I immediately agree.

"Let's just keep her calm. I think that's the best way forward. No excitement or anything to get her riled up."

"Uh..." I say, thinking of my plan to pretend to sell her on the black market. With Darron so frazzled, I decide to not share this with him. "Sure," I agree, "We'll have a quiet afternoon. Maybe have Vanna take us for a little drive if she gets sick of staring at the same walls." I feel guilty lying to Darron, but if Nico is right and having Shauna help out gives her the sort of purpose that will keep her on the straight and narrow, then it will all be for the best in the end.

Darron gives my hands a little squeeze. "Better get that tea out to her; she needs a steady drip drip drip of sugar to keep her mood leveled out."

"Gotcha."

"I should be back no later than eight o'clock," he adds.

"Then we can work together to get her settled for the night," I say. "I'll call Kimmy and see if she can maybe get us some animal tranquilizers to get us both a chance to sleep tonight." As a half-vamp Shauna doesn't sleep, but we both know she can be knocked out.

Normally this is the type of thing Darron would frown upon. "Friends don't drug friends," he would say. But as a testament to the day he's undergone, he simply nods and says, "Good plan."

And with that, he's out the door, moving a little faster than his usual pace, like he can't get away fast enough.

And I'm left with sugar hungry semi-sober Shauna.

11

Kimmy and Jax stop by to check on Shauna and drop off some tranquilizers along with a cooler of blood. I don't think I've ever been so glad to see Jax, even when we were "happily" married. I take the break to use the bathroom and have some alone time. Even if it's only twenty minutes.

Shauna oscillates between being basically catatonic to being a bundle of energy. At first I thought I could put her bursts of activity to use. I had her fly up to the roof to clean the gutters, but ended up losing a bunch of roof tiles when Shauna decided to see how far she could throw them. Spoiler alert—as far as the edge of the yard. Now my property line is littered with roof tiles.

When I come back out of the bathroom, Jax and Kimmy are edging toward the door. "And when will we see you again?" I ask desperately.

"Well, we're pretty busy," Jax says, ready to climb out the window.

I lower my voice. "Shauna is your sister..." How did I get into a weird custody situation with my ex's sister?!

"We'll help!" Kimmy promises.

"Yes, we'll help," Jax echoes. "I'll text you my availability," he says as he disappears through the window, his wings sprouting for a moment to help him balance.

"I won't hold my breath," I mutter.

Kimmy gives me a smile. "I'll nudge him," she tells me. "He's just not very good when things get hard."

"Oh, believe me, I'm aware." I walk her to the door. Jax is waiting for her on the walk.

"Keep Shauna fed," Kim tells me. "I brought a ton of blood, but let me know if you need more."

"Thanks. I can't pay you…" I trail off.

"Our treat!" Kimmy says. She's so blonde and perky and perfect. And still, I like her.

I wave goodbye, then go to make Shauna a blood shake, with just a few scoops of sugar. While I'm at it, my phone rings. It's Canwella.

"Paige! My mole at Au Naturale says something is going on tonight there. Something big. It might be a good time to check things out."

"I'm on it!" I tell her.

"Should I tell him to set up a buy? You and the fae girl, right?"

I look at the blood concoction in front of me. And the bottle of tranquilizers. "Let me text you right back," I tell her.

In the living room, Shauna is cuddling Shit, who looks like he desperately wants to get away from her.

"Shauna," I hand her the blood shake. A few gulps and she mellows out. "I have something to ask you."

"Shoot," she says.

"I know it's a bad time, but…were you really with the FBI?"

"What? Is that so hard to believe?" she asks as she slurps up her blood shake.

I take a deep breath. "I need to go undercover at a seedy brothel and I need to pose as a supe trafficker. But I also need a supe to traffic."

"I'm in," she tells me, leaping to her feet.

"I'm not done explaining," I say.

"Doesn't matter. I'm in. Whatever you need. I'm going crazy over here, without beauty, without sugar. I feel like I want to scratch off my own skin. Without beauty I'm just awake. It's just me, with me, twenty-four seven. It's the worst."

"About that..." I put the bottle of tranqs down on the table. "Kimmy brought these. She said two should get you at least a few hours of sleep."

She sits back down, staring at the bottle. "A few hours of oblivion?" She looks at her blood shake. "You didn't...."

"No, I wouldn't just drug you without your consent. I mean, not unless it was worst case." I shake the bottle. "I'm giving you a choice. Come with me, or go get some sleep."

"Is this field trip with Nico?" she asks.

"No, Nico isn't invited. The place knows him. He'd just get in the way." I explain. It's also totally payback for him not taking me to the Monarch Club, but whatever. I don't need him. I can figure this out on my own.

"Then I'm coming with you." She eyes the bottle of pills a little regretfully. "To help."

"Are you sure?"

"Shit yeah, I'm sure!" she shouts. Shit raises his head at his name, then tries to burrow into the couch pillows.

"Great. Yes. Let me get the details and we'll go."

"RIDE OR DIE!!!" Shauna shouts, pops into her pixie form, then does loopty loops around the room.

I text Canwella for the details and then go to raid Darron's extensive closet.

Somehow a drag queen has exactly what I think a supe trafficker would wear—knee high black boots and a bright red wraparound. When I come out of his room Shauna gives me a once over.

"Who's for sale, me or you?" she asks with a smirk.

"Shut it," I warn her. "Or I'll go bargain basement on your price tag."

12

———

Super Au Natural is exactly what I expected. The windows are tinted too dark to see inside, but the blinking neon lights leave no doubt as to what is behind the door. Different supe creatures cycle through an array of sexual positions, flashing blue, green, red, and pink.

"I can't even identify half of them," I say under my breath, as I make a preventative grab for the hand sanitizer in Vanna's glove box.

"The supes or what they're doing?" Shauna asks, narrowing her eyes at the neon lights as they begin a fresh run-through of the various activities advertised within. "Because the first one is—"

"I'm good, thanks," I say, checking my reflection in the mirror before popping the door. I hate myself for it. Do I really care about how I look when walking into this place?

"Ready?" I ask Shauna, who gives me a nod as we cross the parking lot.

"Remember," I tell her. "You're drugged."

Shauna winces. "I don't understand why I have to

pretend. I mean, why not just let me take a hit of beauty as soon as I walk in the door? I'm sure there will be plenty of opportunity, and these are dire times...an exception."

"Dire times?" I stop and confront her, hands on my hips. "You've been clean for one day!"

"One. Long. Dire. Damn. Day," she deadpans.

"No. Sorry," I tell her, as I push through Au Naturale's front door, only to face an entryway and another tinted door. Apparently glances aren't even free here. "I'm not going to be the reason you fall off the wagon. I guess you'll just have to dig deep into your previous experiences and try some method acting."

"Oh! Darron told me all about that," she says. "I've been practicing." Her face suddenly goes slack, and her eyes lose focus. I've got to admit, it's convincing. I'm about to compliment her when a heavy hand falls on my shoulder.

"Members only," a highly melodic voice greets me, and I turn to face Canwella's mole—the ogre bouncer.

Canwella and Romy had prepared me for this, but I've never seen a male ogre in person. He's massive. If Canwella is a hill then this guy is a mountain. A mountain with muscles. Everything on him bulges, and I have to admit that I take a sneak peek to confirm that yes—everything does in fact, bulge.

"Wow," Shauna says, her eyes most certainly focused again—and like mine they went right to his package.

"Sorry, we're not members, but we're here to do the dishes," I tell him, repeating the phrase that Canwella had said to use in order to identify myself.

The ogre nods once, then clicks off an earpiece so that our words aren't relayed inside. "Bob," he says, offering a hand.

"Bob?" I repeat, surprised. Most supe names verge on the ridiculous. I've never met one with such a simple one.

"Short for Bobalanga," he clarifies.

"Good move on going with Bob," I say, shaking his hand. My fingers are tiny in his, like toothpicks surrounded by hot dogs.

I should stop thinking about wieners. I nudge Shauna to redirect her attention. "It's not polite to stare," I remind her. "Also, you're drugged."

"Right, yep," she agrees, snapping back into somnolent mode.

"Harmargan is in his office, downstairs," Bob informs us. "You'll need a password to get below. It changes every day, so don't try to use this again. Today's password is *engorged*."

"That's disgusting," I say.

"Yesterday it was *flaccid*," Bob says with a shrug.

"I doubt that," Shauna says, eyes back on his crotch.

"You armed?" Bob asks, and I shake my head. Canwella had already warned me that I didn't dare try to walk into Au Naturale packing heat. The last person that went in there with a weapon walked out without it...and one less hand.

"Alright, ladies," Bob says, clicking his headset back on and performing a perfunctory search on us for the benefit of the security cameras. "You know the drill, first floor looks are free, but if you want to get close enough to touch—or smell—you've got to dish out the dollars."

I want to say "disgusting" again, but I realize I'm supposed to be a member, and beyond that, a trafficker. Paige Harper, supe trafficker, wouldn't have a problem with some supernatural sex sniffing.

I square my shoulders and brace myself before pushing open the darkened door.

Inside is no surprise, but I still have to work hard to keep my head from spinning. Completely nude supes stroll around, both on the stage and on the floor. A young satyr slides past us, holding out a tray of glowing pink drinks. I wave him off, and pull back Shauna's hand as she goes to touch him.

"No. Beauty." I remind her.

"But he's so prettttttyyyy," she whines, and I squeeze her hand tighter, feeling the small bones in it.

"For Tina," I whisper.

Proving I've chosen the right chain to yank, Shauna's mouth goes into a thin line and her drugged act kicks back in.

Hopefully I don't have to remind her too many more times what's at stake here. I can't imagine what would happen if we get busted...but I get a possible clue when I spot a vamp tending bar who is sporting a collar around her neck.

Shauna has told me about them before. It's a collar that strips supes of their abilities. This vamp, for example, can't levitate now. She serves a drink to a customer, and when she tells them their total her lips can't hide the fact that she's been defanged.

"Shit," I breathe to myself. I don't know what this employee did to be punished, but no one can claim she's here of her own free will. I steady myself and make my way to the bar, sliding onto a stool. Shauna takes the one beside me, eyeing the vamp bartender.

"What's good here?" I ask the vamp. I'm not ready to descend to another level yet. Just the antics on the stage are enough to make me queasy.

"To drink or...?" The vamp asks, what's supposed to be a devilish grin not quite succeeding. She just looks depressed.

"To drink," I say firmly, just as a fae onstage yelps when

her pole partner—a heavily muscled incubus—slaps her rear end with a black riding crop. A welt raises immediately, and money rains onto the stage from the human customers.

"We've got ambrosia...watered down for humans, of course," the vamp says, returning Shauna's stare. "What's your problem?"

"She's...with me," I say, clamping a hand onto Shauna's wrist. "And she's for sale," I add.

The vamp's expression changes entirely, her somewhat welcoming eyes darkening into cold stones. "Ambrosia, and basically anything else a human bar would offer," she says. "That's what I've got."

"I'll take a beer, thanks," I say, hoping that at least if I'm a supe trafficker I can win points by being a polite one. Apparently not. My beer is plopped down in front of me so hard that a head rises and spills over the top. The vamp turns her back to me, madly polishing a non-existent spot on the bar.

I spin on my stool to take in the crowd. Most of the customers are humans and male, but there is the occasional female gawker, and a few supes that aren't employees. It's easy to tell because they're actually wearing clothes. All of the supes that work here are young...really young. It's not always easy to pin an age on them—and virtually impossible with vamps—but one of the naked succubi firmly planted on the lap of a human still has baby fat on her cheeks.

I feel ill. I don't want my beer, and I don't want to be here any longer than necessary. Beside me, Shauna twitches, moving my hand from her wrist to encircle her fingers with mine. I give her a squeeze—a more friendly one this time—just as I spot a well-dressed businessman duck through a curtain of beads that leads to a back hallway. A flashing light above the doorway declares it "EXXXTRA: CASH ONLY."

I change my mind and down my beer in two gulps, then wipe my mouth on my arm. "Let's get this over with," I say to Shauna.

The beer hits me faster than expected and I stumble a little on the way to the back. A hand catches me and rights me, a pleasant-faced dude gives me a smile. "Careful," he says. "The floors in here are slick."

On a normal day, in a normal place, this guy would be considered polite, maybe even charming. But he's a human who paid to be here, inside of this horrible place.

"Fuck you," I spit at him, and jerk my arm away.

I'm still pissed off when I hit the beaded curtains, dragging Shauna behind. So when two harpies stand shoulder to shoulder, blocking my way, I'm far from polite.

"I've got a fae to sell and I'll go low to get her off my hands," I say. "She's a rude, selfish little shit of an addict and has broken three TVs."

"Hey!" Shauna objects as the harpies exchange a glance.

"And the password is *engorged*," I go on. "Now get the fuck out of my way so I can do some business."

The harpies slide apart like elevator doors to reveal a set of stairs leading down into darkness. I toss my hair and walk past them like I've done this a thousand times.

But I haven't.

And I'm terrified.

13

We pass a few private rooms that can hardly be called that—some of the doors are cracked and I see things that make me wish my vagina would instantly grow shut. A few customers wander the halls, sneaking peeks and paying for it with large bills when the ogres who monitor the hall decide it's time for them to pay up. Shauna and I slide past them, and I fervently wish my ears would grow shut as well. Behind me, I can hear Shauna breathing hard, her temper surely rising.

"Hang on," I say under my breath. "We're almost there."

At the end of the hall stands one last ogre bouncer, this one bigger than the others and with barely a flicker of intelligence in his eyes. I don't bother introducing myself, or even stringing together a sentence for him. I just give the password and he moves aside, unblocking a door that's marked OFFICE.

I walk in, Shauna trailing behind, to find a cyclops sitting behind a huge desk, flanked by another set of harpies.

"Harmargan?" I ask, trying to hold eye contact.

Somehow Nico makes one eye seem sexy as hell. This cyclops was born that way and can't pull it off.

He nods. "My bartender says you're here to sell?"

Shit, is everyone in this place wired?

"Yeah," I agree, pulling Shauna in front of me. "Caught this one and I'm looking to dump her. She's nothing but trouble." Realizing this is a terrible sales pitch, I add, "But she's cute and looks—" I'm about to say young, because that's clearly what they prize here, but the word sticks in my throat. "Pink," I fill in after an awkwardly loud pause.

Harmargan rises from behind his desk, his huge bulk skirting around it gracefully. No wonder he doesn't have more ogre bodyguards in here—there isn't room for them. And besides, I know from experience that harpies can be mean as hell, and it looks like he's got these two hopped on their drug of choice—meth. Their eyes skitter and dance over Shauna and me, looking for any excuse to come at us and tear our hair out.

"Trouble, huh?" Harmargan asks, sliding around Shauna to get a good look at her from behind. "I've got some customers who pay extra if you'll give them a little trouble."

Shauna stiffens, the blood rising in her face.

He takes a chunk of her hair and gives it a little tug. I hold my breath, hoping Shauna can resist reacting. "Pink," he says. "It is that." He paws at her shirt with his oversized hands, like he might pull it right off her. "Or is she talking about some other pink parts?"

"Seems like a decent source of income," I say, jerking Shauna closer to me and out of his grasp. "I'm new at this, human—I mean supe—trafficking, but I bet I could make a good bit on the side."

"You could make more than a bit," Harmargan agrees,

and I realize now he's checking *me* out. I spin on my heel, glaring at him.

"I am not for sale," I inform him.

He shrugs, his one eye still devouring me. "Maybe a consideration for the future, then, if this line of work doesn't pan out for you. I've got a stake in an all-human place across town. It doesn't do the kind of business we do, of course, but it's not nothing either."

Harmargan goes back to his desk, giving Shauna's wings a flick on the way. A barely controlled squeak of rage slips past her lips.

"How'd you hear about me?" Harmargan asks, leaning back in his chair and crossing his hands behind his head. I take a risk and float the only story I could come up with in the parking lot.

"Canwella," I tell him. "I tried to sell this little pixie to her, but she said Charms only operates on the up and up. She was tossing me out by my ears and said I should give Harmargan a call, that Super Au Naturale doesn't ask questions."

"Ah, Canwella," he says, with a genuine smile. "Always liked that girl. No head for business, what with keeping everything moral and all, but I have to hand it to her. Running a clean place and keeping it afloat is a lot harder than what I do."

"Um...yeah," I agree. I was totally unprepared for him to show what appears to be real admiration for the ogre madame. I wonder what their deal is. But I can't forget why I'm here.

"It's especially hard to stay in business when you get robbed," I add.

"What?" Harmargan asks, leaning forward now. "Somebody robbed the old girl?"

Beside me, Shauna almost chokes. Harmargan's reaction is genuinely gleeful. Maybe he's acting, but why bother? He doesn't know me, why pretend? Now his face widens into a grin.

"She kept that pretty secret. That Canwella, always keeping her cards close to her vest." He clearly wants to gloat over this new information I've given him, and that's all I need to know to realize that we're in the wrong place...and in the middle of selling Shauna to a skin dealer.

"Yeah, I was there when it happened so that's how I know about it." Shit, did I just mess up Canwella's plan? If she didn't want anyone to know, she should have told me.

"Was it the same person that hit the Monarchs?" Harmargan asks, his temper rising now. "I tell you—somebody's got it in for honest supe business people."

"Honest?" Shauna yells, no longer able to contain herself. "You've got girls and boys working up there that barely just crawled out of their mommas!"

Harmargan shrugs, spreading his hands wide. "They're safer here than they are out in the human world."

"What about the collars?" Shauna dives for the desk, her two small fists pounding it. "That's punishment! That's inhumane! That's what they used to do at Underworld Reformatory!"

On either side of Harmargan, the harpies come to attention, their wings spreading out, eyes burning with an inner light.

"Yes," Harmargan says, his own gaze now changing to something more sinister as he takes a second look at Shauna. "Underworld Reformatory, that's where my harpies are from. They were the guards there, right?"

"Yes!" Shauna yells, and her wings vibrate—a sure sign

she's about to snap into pixie mode and obliterate something.

"You know what, I think I've changed my mind," I say lightly. "Maybe I'll...just open my own brothel. No collars. Only hand jobs."

Harmargan's eyebrow flies up, but it's the best I've got at the moment. I edge towards the door, tugging on Shauna's sleeve.

"You're not going anywhere," Harmargan says, and his harpies begin to weave back and forth, ready for a command. "I thought I recognized her," he says, pointing to Shauna. "You were on TV!"

"Yeah, I'm famous, so what?" Shauna snaps, but he cuts her off.

"Tell me why you and a"–his eyes flick to me–"human hooker are in my establishment?"

"I'm not a hooker," I say, and make a dash for the door. But a harpy stops me, her bony claws circling my wrist and not letting go. She forces me to my knees, bending my arm painfully behind me.

"You don't know poop about me!" Shauna cries. "I'm a fae vampire and I'm going to drink you dry."

Shauna pops into her pixie form and does a loop of the room to get up speed. She's about to hit Harmagan right in the middle of his bulbous eye when he holds open a glass jar. A glowing glass jar.

Shauna, like other pixies, is attracted to bright lights. She also has the attention span of a gnat so she heads straight for it. Once she's inside, Harmagan pops on the lid and puts the glass jar on his desk. Shauna panically flits around the jar but can't get out.

She pounds on the jar with her tiny hands, her little

mouth open in a shout I can't hear. Harmagan holds it up and laughs, shaking it slightly.

"Don't!" I shout.

"A little pixie vamp hybrid might draw some crowds. But you know what? I know exactly who wants to get first crack at this little mosquito." He tosses Shauna's jar down on the desk and grabs his phone. Shauna kicks at the glass until she realizes it's useless. She slumps to the bottom, arms folded over her knees.

I really screwed the pooch on this one. I put Shauna in danger, just when she was trying to get her life back on track. Plus this whole thing was a dead end.

"Yeah, I know you said to never call you but I got someone here you're gonna want to see. No. I don't care. Look, he's gonna want to get his hands dirty for this one. Just tell him, okay." He hangs up the phone and focuses on me.

"Now you...' Harmargan says, kneeling down to face me. "I don't know who you think you are, coming in here and trying to pull one over on me. But I'm going to find out. And I'm going to make you pay."

14

I don't want to know the methods by which Harmargan means to get the truth out of me, but I'm willing to bet it's not going to be pretty. He kneels in front of me, gazing into my eyes, one fist tucked under his chin as he considers what specific torture to put me through.

"My customers are here for supes," he says, tracing my jawline with one finger. "But I bet I could find someone on the floor interested in seeing what's under that dress."

"If anyone touches me, I swear..." I try to play it tough, but the truth is, I'm scared. I've dealt with some bad guys before, but from what I've seen out there—this is next level. These people are without conscience. So when Harmargan talks about throwing me to his customers like a piece of raw meat, I know he's not bluffing.

"If anyone touches you...what?" he asks, a greasy smile on his face. He knows I'm powerless and he likes it. Hell, he almost seems to be getting off on it.

My mind spins desperately, searching for a way out of this. If I could get a message to Canwella or Nico...

Then I see it, right as Harmargan pulls his hand back

from my face. He's wearing a huge ring, a massive ruby and diamond "O" with the year on the side—the last year Ohio State University football won the college championship game. I only know because Jax lost our car on a bet that night.

"Ohio," I say, raising my chin in defiance, and Harmargan's eyes snap away from my cleavage.

"What?"

"Ohio," I say again, my heart beating way too fast as I try to pull the meaning of that acronym from the far recesses of my brain. "You're a member of O.H.I.O—the Order for Human Improvement Options. Your whole business is a front for it." I don't know this for sure, but he grimaces at my words, so I think I hit a nerve.

"And I'm telling you that if anyone lays a finger on me, or this pixie, Brent Anders will find out about it—and he won't be happy." *Please let this be true*, I silently add.

Harmargan rocks back on his heels, reconsidering me. "How do you know Senator Anders?"

"I was almost Mrs. Anders," I tell him, more confident now as Harmargan is no longer crowding me. "And while I may not be his wife, he's not exactly going to like it if his former girlfriend is passed around by his underlings."

Harmargan stands up, leaning against the desk, studying me like something doesn't add up.

"Bullshit. You're cute but you're no senator's wife."

Ouch, that hurts. Mostly because he's right. Before I knew that Brent was a murderous bastard, the thing that held me back from making our relationship official was knowing I'd never truly fit into the politician's wife mold.

But I don't need to go into all that with this asshole.

"Google me," I tell him. "Paige Harper. I run a supernatural cleaning service."

Harmargan whips out his phone, and after a few taps and a couple seconds of scrolling, he flicks his finger at the harpies. I'm released. I rub at my arm, trying to hide the trembles that come with the knowledge of how close I came to being—my mind shies away from finishing that thought. I'm sure my nightmares tonight, though, will fill in for me what would've happened if I'd been tossed to the human wolves that make up Harmargan's customer base.

"Are we free to go?" I ask, pushing myself to my feet and pretending a confidence I'm nowhere close to feeling.

"Not yet," Harmargan says. "You say Senator Anders won't like it if any harm comes to you, but you'd be surprised what some men like."

He punches some numbers on his phone and I swallow, hard. I was hoping Brent's name would be enough to call off the dogs...because even Nico Tralano won't be able to sniff me out if I don't come back from this.

"Call him," I say, lifting my chin high, like I'm insulted he thinks this won't go my way.

"I already did," he leans back, puts his feet on his desk, and motions for me to sit.

"You...?" Oh my god. I'm an idiot. The person Harmargan just offered "first crack" at Shauna to was Brent. I don't know why I'm surprised. I already knew he was capable of murder, and what with Canwella's comment about Firsters often wanting to be first in line for supe sex... but still.

It's amazing that my exes can still find ways to disappoint me. No, this is way beyond disappointment. The things that happen here...there's no way Brent's unaware.

My stomach turns with the realization that I once slept with a guy who does business with human traffickers. And, you know, murders people on occasion.

Harmargan picks his smartphone up from his desk, looks at it a moment and then back to me. "Maybe I should call him back. Update him that there's another lady here—" he says lady so it sounds like an insult, "he might be interested in. I'd be interested in knowing how Senator Andres reacts to finding out his ex-fianceé is here. Does he shit a brick?"

Not wanting to let him know that there's a chance Brent might not care at all, I shrug and say, "If you know Brent then you know he doesn't wear his heart on his sleeve."

"He guards his heart, sure," Harmargan agrees. "But he can't hide his BMs. Not from me anyway."

"Um...what?" I honestly can't tell if this is some weird double-entendre that's going right over my head. But in my world, BM stands for only one thing. Bowel movement.

"My IT girl dosed him with a sort of magic tapeworm that lives in his belly. Every time he takes a dump, it emits a signal."

My eyes widen in horror. I slept with Brent. "Can he transfer it to other people?"

Harmargan grins at me, like he knows exactly what I'm thinking. "Nah, it's happy where it is. Anyway, it'd get pretty confusing if we were tracking dumps from everyone he gets close to."

Ew. But also, "And how does it help you, knowing where Brent leaves his number twos?"

"It helps me keep tabs on him. They say a man doesn't shit where he eats, but there's not a coffee shop in this town he hasn't defecated in."

I frown, trying to see the usefulness in knowing this information. I mean, it's useless if he's constipated or even if he's just not pooping anywhere important. "I guess if you wanted to catch him with his pants down..."

"That's it exactly!" Harmargan exclaims. "And trust me, he's got his own ways of keeping an eye on me, I'm sure of it." Harmargan shrugs. "In this business it's dog eat dog." He laughs. "The best part is, he has no idea we're tracking him. As a decoy we put something in his car; he found it within a few weeks and thought that was it. Like that was our only attempt." A new gleam comes to Harmargan's eyes. "Paige Harper, you said your name was?"

"Yeah." I don't like the way he's looking at me, like he's figuring out all my weaknesses. But then I haven't liked any part of being in this man's orbit.

"You got a cleaning business, which makes you a cleaning lady."

I narrow my eyes at him. He's the type to immediately imagine me in a French maid outfit and I don't want him going there. "I've been known to scrub a shitter or two."

He nods, pleased by this. "It's you!" An evil chuckle erupts from deep within him. "When we had the tracker in his car, we got these recordings of him moaning to someone, about the one who got away. The cleaning lady. That's what he called you." Another laugh comes, this one more sinister than the first. "You must have some sort of magic twat."

"Actually, Brent always said he loves my sparkling personality," I counter. It's true…ish. Brent used to say he didn't like ballsy women, but I was the exception. At the time it made me feel special. Now, reflecting, I just feel like an idiot for not taking that as the warning it was. Of course he didn't like strong women. Of course it could never work out between us.

"Ha, ha, that was a lie," Harmargan says dismissively, like the idea of anyone seeing another person as more than just a sex hole is ridiculous. "You gotta hear this for yourself. I'm sure we still got the recording somewhere. Let me get Hepatitis in here."

"No, that's okay. I'm good," I say, because I don't want to hear this recording or have anything to do with hepatitis.

But Harmargan doesn't give a shit what I want. He leans a bit to the left and knocks on a door that I'd assumed was a closet. "Come out, come out, little witch." He grins at me. "You're gonna be impressed," he assures me. "I got the best tech witch in the business."

"Fuck you," comes a voice from behind the door. Just as I look over, the door flies open revealing a...closet. Just as I suspected. But this closet has a tiny desk, a single hanging bulb, and a normal sized person crammed into it. An angry person. Her eyes spark as she glares at Harmargan in a way that promises vengeance. I hope she gets it...although with the collar around her neck it might be difficult.

"Hepatitis," Haramargan chides. "Be polite. We have guests."

She shows him double middle fingers.

Harmargan just laughs. "Four years here and she's still feisty as ever." He glances to Hepatitis. "Looks like you're due for another break." For a moment I'm relieved that she at least gets to occasionally escape that cramped closet, but then Harmargan continues, "What should it be this time? Crack that thigh bone in half again? It's great because she studied to be a healer, so she can just heal herself right up!"

He says this like it's a big joke, but from the way Hepatitis goes pale, I can see it's a very real threat.

"I'm doing the work," she says in a more subdued voice.

Harmargan shrugs. "Yeah, yeah, you're doing the work, but you're getting mouthy again." He looks to me. "I'd off her, but she's magic with electronics and tech stuff. She's a witch. Most of 'em don't like tech. Stupid old school supe thing. But she's got all of that electro stuff under her spell."

I turn to Hepatitis who still glares at Harmargan. "I'm sorry," I say to her. Meaning, I'm sorry she's stuck here with this gross man.

I close my eyes. And now I'm stuck here too.

15

———

The door to the office opens and the huge bouncer ogre sticks his head in. "Boys in blue are here. Say they want double this month." He rubs his fingers together in the universal sign for money.

Boys in blue can only be the cops. Desperately, my mind spins, wondering if there's some way I can get a message to them. But would they even help me when they're obviously here to collect bribes? It'd be tough for them to save me at the same time they're taking bribes to look the other way.

Meanwhile, Harmargan reaches into his desk and extracts a thick wad of cash, all the while grumbling *"breaking my balls"* and *"remind them I got dirt on them too."* Then he tells the harpies to stay on guard before heading out the door.

I look to the harpies with my best smile. "Any chance you want to let me go in exchange for me cleaning your homes gratis? Home cleaning on the house, you could say, if you like a little play on words."

They look at me with dead eyes. Clearly not fans of winning smiles or clever word play.

Okay then. I turn to Hepatitis. "I don't suppose you've got any sway around here?"

She points to the collar around her neck. "What do you think?"

Right. Then I can't help but ask, "Uh, is that your actual name?"

She sighs heavily, like she's heard this question too many times before. "My friends call me Hepa. But I'm not among friends here."

She looks so sad now, almost beaten except for that spark still burning in the back of her eyes. I hope she gets free. I hope they all do. The fact that this place exists and that everyone seems to know and just accept it. I guess it's naive of me to be surprised. It's not like I didn't know bad shit existed in the world. But seeing it up close like this...I can't imagine ever shaking it off.

"It's how things go sometimes." She shrugs. "Old story, really. Decided to dabble in a little black magic and it didn't go well."

In her jar I can see Shauna nodding as if to agree she's heard that one before.

"I'm sorry," I say again, even though it seems like nowhere near enough in these circumstances. Leaning in closer to her, I lower my voice. "You've been here four years...is there anyone I can contact for you?"

She hesitates, then shakes her head. "I burned a few bridges. No one cares or they would have come for me already."

"That can't be true," I assure her. "And now I know you're here. And I'm sure as shit not sticking around. Is there anyone who can bring this place down?"

Hepa shakes her head. "Anyone powerful enough to take

it down is either on Harmargan's payroll or has bigger fish to fry."

"Oh." I sigh. "I'm—"

Hepa rolls her eyes. "Don't tell me you're sorry again. I get it. We're all sorry, but it is what it is."

"My client, Canwella, she owns a supe brothel, but a nice one—"

"I know who she is," Hepa interrupts.

"She says they've gotten people out before. I could ask her—"

Hepa shuts this down before I can even finish talking. "They've raided us a few times to scoop up some naive young thing. Afterwards Harmargan ups his defenses and makes it more difficult the next time. No one's gonna waste a chance on me. And they shouldn't. I can take care of myself. Besides it's kind of amusing convincing Harmargan that the best way to track someone is through their bowel movements."

I can't help but laugh. "That was your idea? It does seem kind of wrong. Like, you know *magic.* Unless you specialize in poop magic. That can't be a thing. Tell me that's not a thing."

"No, it's definitely not. But it's hilarious to watch Harmargan get excited when one of his marks is taking a shit." She hesitates and then adds, begrudgingly, "And thanks, for wanting to help. It helps having a reminder some decent people are left."

Am I a decent person? If I'd heard about this place a year ago, I'm pretty certain I would've shrugged and considered it a supe problem. In other words, not something for me to worry about.

But that's not me anymore. "If—when—I get out of here, I'm going to get this place shut down."

"Just like that?" Hepa asks, her look incredulous.

"Knowing my life, no, it won't be just like that. It will be extremely difficult and I'll probably find out some shit I never wanted to know, like my dad was really Darth Vader..." Or my boyfriend is really the vampire serial killer. "But I'm going to do it."

Hepa darts a glance at the harpies and then says in a quick low voice, "Harmargan's afraid of the Monarchs. If you can somehow use them as leverage—"

Before she can finish, Harmargan bursts through the door. He takes one look at me and Hepa close together. Grabbing her arm he tosses her in the direction of the closet.

"That's enough out of you," Harmargan says, and he slams the closet door closed in Hepa's face. The room is silent for a long moment. Harmargan sighs and shifts like he's uncomfortable when he's not tormenting someone. Then his gaze falls on the jar holding Shauna.

"This one..." Harmargan clicks his long dirty nails against Shauna's jar. "She was the one that attacked him before he was elected, right? Literally tore him a new asshole."

"No, not literally," I interrupt him, even though I get the idea he's the type who doesn't like to be cut off when he's monologuing. But honestly, I just can't. Does no one know what the word literally means anymore?

Predictably, Harmargan's eyes narrow. "Whatever," he says, "I'm not a grammarian or his doctor, but she did beat him up. That's for sure. And he's not the bygones type. I figure he'd love a little alone time with her."

"In her defense, he did kill her brother," I say.

"That attack boosted him to political stardom," Harmargan says. From somewhere on his desk, he finds a toothpick. It looks used. Almost...fuzzy. But he sticks it in his mouth and starts picking at his teeth. I swallow hard, fairly certain that vomiting all over his floor won't help my cause. "That little pixie going after him is why he got elected."

"On a Human's First ticket!" I cry, unable to believe this guy. "How can you support someone who hates you?"

Harmargan laughs. "Everyone hates me. I don't care. As long as I can do what I love and get paid to do it."

"You're disgusting," I tell him, spitting out the words.

"And you're a judgy bitch," he shoots back. "I wonder how much Senator Anders will pay for you..."

"Nothing," a familiar voice says behind me. I turn.

But it's not Brent at the door, ready to save me once again to prove he's a hero.

It's his current girlfriend, long time lapdog, and partner in crime, Giselle.

"Fuck my life," both she and I say at the same time. Cleary, neither of us is happy to see the other.

"I should have known," Giselle says, tossing her red mane of hair as she steps into Harmargan's office. "Anytime there's trouble in Brent's life, you're at the bottom of it.

"Works both ways," I tell her, my voice steely.

Harmargan leans back in his chair, enjoying the show. Inside her jar, Shauna zips to life at the sight of Giselle, screaming silent obscenities and finally settling for some good old fashioned hand gestures when she realizes no one can hear her.

"Seriously, how low can you go?" I ask Giselle as she perches on the side of Harmargan's desk. "Your boyfriend sends you to pick up his next murder victim?"

"A couple of corrections," Giselle says airily. "Fiancé, not boyfriend." She waves a diamond under my nose, close enough for it to almost slice my face. "And secondly, the atmosphere must have gone to your head, Paige. Brent is many things, but he is not a murderer."

"He is literally a murderer," I shout.

"I'm here to collect this trollop so that Brent can have an honest heart to heart with her," she continues, ignoring me. "He feels dreadful about the death of her brother, and wants to make sure there are no hard feelings...as well as an understanding that he had nothing to do with it."

Behind her, Harmargan mouths "bullshit" to me, then sticks his index finger into a hole he makes with his other hand.

"I'm not going to stand here and argue with you about which one of us is delusional," I tell her, crossing my arms.

"And I'm not going to stand here much longer at all," Giselle announces, sweeping Shauna's jar off her desk and into her purse. "My job here is done."

"Wait! You're leaving me!" I shout, for the first time in my life wanting to be around Giselle more. "You can't just—"

Harmargan's phone rings—his tone is apparently "'Don't Worry, Be Happy." He lets it play for a second, nodding along with the tune before answering.

"Boss man," he says, then with one of those nasty chuckles his attention turns back to me. "You're in everyone's hearts and minds today, it seems." His smile freezes in place at whatever Brent is saying.

"You're sure?" Harmargan asks. Then, getting up with a huge sigh, hands me his phone. "He wants to talk to you."

"To her?" Giselle asks, her nose scrunching up in disbelief.

I take the phone, grateful for any port in a storm. "Brent?"

"Paige," he says calmly. "Why are you in the backroom of the most disgusting brothel in the city?"

"Why are you on the manager's speed dial?" I snap back, then realize something. "How did you know I was here?"

"Your right hand was just in the frame of the photo Harmargan sent me," he says. "I'd know that hand anywhere." Oh god. I look down at my hand and the tattoo on the back of my wrist. I got it after my parents ghosted. It's the constellation Ursa Minor.

My parents used to love to tell the story of their first date. My dad took my mom out to look at the stars. All he knew was the big and little dipper, so he made up names for the others. Mom decided to give him shit, said he should've done his homework before bringing her out there. My dad was always quick on his feet. He said that he figured knowing Ursa Minor was the bear minimum, anything beyond that was gravy. Ever since then Ursa Minor was theirs.

The tat's been on my hand for so long now, I sometimes forget it's even there. But clearly it hasn't faded from Brent's mind.

"You know, I still have the video," he says, his voice low and rough. I'm about to ask what video, when I remember. He once convinced me to let him capture on his phone a short clip of me jerking him off. I agreed so long as it was just dick and my hands. I guess a part of me always knew better than to trust him with anything more than that. "You need to delete that," I tell him now.

"I don't think so," he says. "You clearly still have uses for me, so it only seems fair that I still get some use out of you."

"No," I say carefully. "That's not how this works." I'm not about to take a stroll down Mating Memory Lane right now with my disgusting ex, but I also can't afford to piss him off. Across from me, Giselle's mouth tightens as she digs her own phone out of her purse, dialing quickly. In my ear, Brent's phone gets a call waiting signal.

"One sec," he says

"Wait," I warn, but it's too late. He picks her up on the other line.

"Brent," she says. "Let Harmargan deal with her once and for all."

I pull Harmargan's phone from my ear and dash off a text to Brent. *"Do you want me to tell her that you propositioned me in the library? AFTER you two were together?"*

"Brent?" Giselle pushes, clearly annoyed at not getting an immediate answer.

Three dots appear after my text message, followed by the surprised face with the big "O" for a mouth. The splash of liquid finishes the message.

"Are you fucking kidding me?" I say aloud.

It's an old joke between the two of us, a mixing of what should be innocent emojis that translate to something intimate and personal. Brent just told me he wants a blowjob in exchange for getting me out of this.

I text back the dead face with X's for eyes.

Fuck him. Or should I say I will never again fuck him.

Or ask for his help.

I'll figure this out myself.

16

———

I delete my messages then toss Harmargan's phone onto the desk, and he dives to grab it before it hits the floor. Maybe I could have called someone before giving it back, but I don't know anyone's numbers off the top of my head, and 911 would be a bust. The cops are already here and they're on Harmargan's payroll.

"Brent??" Giselle asks again into her own phone, a line of worry between her eyebrows. "What do you want me to do?"

"Probably blow him," I tell her, then turn to Harmargan. "Look," I say, "I'm done pretending. I came here because I thought maybe you were the one behind the robbery at Charms. Turns out you're not. Me being a skin dealer and Shauna being for sale was all just a cover to get us down here."

"Uh-huh, I put that together myself," Harmargan says. "What's your point? Am I supposed to be like oh, your little gambit failed, but it was cute! Ta ta, girls!"

"No," I say, squaring my shoulders. "You're supposed to let me go—and give Shauna back—because if you don't I'll let the Monarchs know you've got a girl up there who looks like she just left her cocoon."

I'd spotted her on one of the poles. A lightly built little thing with a tasteful butterfly tattoo on her shoulder blade. She moved so gracefully that the tat looked like it could take wing right off her skin.

"What?" Giselle asks, finally distracted from her phone. "A monarch like, a ruler?"

The light goes out of Harmargan's eyes, and his smile tightens. "You're awfully observant. But did you also see she had no collar around her neck? That means the girl is here of her own free will."

"The Monarchs won't care about that. They hate this place as much as Canwella does. Maybe even more. If they knew one of their own kind is working here, I can't see them being happy about it," I say, hoping like hell I'm right. And that Hepa was right too with her tip about Harmargan being afraid of the Monarchs.

Canwella didn't actually say as much, but if there's one thing I've learned about the supe world, it's that each species looks after their own. Also, she was the only shifter out there in human form. That tells me she's keeping her butterfly wings for behind closed doors. Maybe that's a way of driving her price up, but I don't think so.

From the crowds out there I think most people come here just to watch and probably can't afford to pay for the more hands-on services. Harmargan wants to keep her hidden in plain sight. Those in the know will get the tattoo signal, and those that aren't don't need to know anyway.

"You can't prove she's a Monarch, and you're not getting out of here to tell anyone anyway," Harmargan smirks, but I can see him starting to sweat.

"The point is," I press on, "that Canwella knew I was

coming here to investigate the robbery, and if I don't come back she'll assume you made me disappear because I caught you out with proof that you were the one who robbed Charms."

Harmargan's smile is completely gone now.

"The Monarchs got hit too, didn't they?" I continue. "You supes are always screwing up human sayings, but here's one you might know…"

I lean over his desk, dropping my voice to a whisper as his one eyeball rolls, taking in my cleavage. "The enemy of my enemy is my friend."

"I get it, I get it," Harmargan says, waving me off. "You don't leave safely, Canwella goes to the Monarchs, they compare notes, assume I'm the thief, and come down here for their revenge, spotting their little flutter-girl."

"And then…" I say, whirling my finger in the air, encouraging him to continue.

"Brent?!?!" Giselle repeats into her phone. "Something's going on…I don't know. Something about blowjobs and butterflies."

"And then Jimmy Monarch comes down on me like a bat out of hell," Harmargan says, raising his one eye to meet mine. "You know what they do to people they don't like?"

"I'm guessing it's not butterfly kisses?"

"They give you a catheter," he says, and both Giselle and I wince.

I was not expecting that. "Dear God, why?" I ask.

"Then they seal you in a cocoon and submerge you in sugar water," he says, considering his possible fate. "It leaks in…slowly. You've got the chance of drinking it fast enough —and draining—out the hole for the catheter. But you can't possibly keep up. Their victims have the choice of drowning…or drinking until your gut explodes."

Wow. Now I understand why Harmargan fears them. There's nothing scarier than when someone gets violently creative.

"Okay, now I just don't even know what's going on," Giselle says to Brent over the phone.

"What's going on is that I'm leaving," I say, straightening up. "And I'm taking Shauna with me."

Giselle drops her phone and gives me a death glare. "You'll do no such thing."

Harmargan gives me a glance, then—with a single crooked finger—the harpies shuffle over to Giselle. She screeches, shying away from their dusty claws.

"Hand the pixie over," Harmargan says. "We can all leave here happily."

Honestly, I don't feel like I can ever be happy again after what I've seen today, but the look on Shauna's face as I twist the lid off the jar almost does the trick. She zips into the open air, snapping into human form.

"Who wants their eyelids ripped off?" she shouts, but I yank on her wrist and she listens—for once.

"Shauna, it's time to go," I tell her. "We get to walk out of here, so let's take that offer and scoot."

"If the cleaning business bottoms out, I've got other work for your bottom!" Harmargan calls after me. "Human or not!"

"Paige! PAIGE!" Giselle comes shooting out of the office right on our heels, clearly terrified to be left alone with Harmargan and the harpies. The three of us take deep breaths and make our way out of Au Naturel by looking straight ahead and trying to ignore our surroundings.

The guy at the bar who'd saved me from a fall earlier gives me an up-nod and tips his beer toward me. "Who's your friend?" he calls, eyes on Giselle.

Normally, I'd never refer to her as my friend, but I don't want to take the time to correct him right now. Or start any kind of conversation. I just want to get out of here...and Giselle does, too. We break out into the sunshine and face off in the parking lot— enemies once more.

"I really like your hair," Shauna tells Giselle. That girl is beyond random. "I hate you with a passion, like you make me vomit into my mouth when I think of you, but you have really great hair."

"Thanks...I guess...what is happening?" Giselle asks. She looks so confused, and who could blame her? Brent is gross and manipulative and I never saw it until he literally tried to kill me.

"Giselle," I say, with a huff. "You don't like me, and I don't like you. But why? Because Brent is my ex? I don't want him back, okay? I'm not interested."

"Then why do you keep showing up in his path?" she asks, cocking a hip and crossing her arms.

"It's more like he's crossing mine...when I'm looking into illegal activities. That should tell you something."

Giselle lifts her chin but doesn't say anything.

"Seriously. Woman to woman now—I've been with a cheater. It sucks. And—" I gesture to the building we just exited. "He's involved with that crap in there."

"For business," Giselle says. "And not by choice, it's part of Oh—" she stops herself before giving away that she was about to say O.H.I.O. Clearing her throat and sticking her nose in the air, she adds, "That's confidential, but please. I would never be with a man who was involved in something this sordid by choice. His work here is...temporary."

Huh. I wonder what that means and what use O.H.I.O. has for Harmargan and his nasty little business. But I can tell I'm not getting anything else out of Giselle. She's all clammed up now. Still, I can't help but try to reach her one more time.

"Would you be with a man who offered to get me out of that mess in exchange for a blow job?" I ask.

"He would never," she says, biting off each word. But I can see a glitter in her eye that wasn't there before. The first hints of a tear?

"He would," I repeat. "Remember what I said to Harmargan? The enemy of my enemy is my friend? We're not friends, Giselle, but one day we might have a common enemy."

I take Shauna by the arm and we head toward Vanna, as Giselle screams after us. "We'll have you for slander, you and your filthy mouth!"

"Hey," Shauna yells, as she climbs into the van. "You're going to want to check that ring for jelly donut residue! I'm telling you, he might have polished it up, but that thing *reeks* of sugar."

"What?" Giselle yells, clearly confused.

"That's how he proposed—" Shauna continues wanting to tell all. But I cut her off.

"Leave it," I shout at Shauna, and Vanna gives her bottom a helpful push with the passenger side door. She tumbles in and we pull away.

"What?" Shauna asks, sitting up and rubbing her head. "I was just going to tell her how Brent hid your ring in a donut, and then apparently he recycled it and just gave it to the next girl."

"I know," I said, my hands tightening on the wheel. I'd recognized my engagement ring on Giselle's finger. But instead of making me mad, I just feel sad...for Giselle.

What I told her was absolutely true. I do know how it feels to be cheated on, and I wouldn't wish it on anyone—even her. But if it does happen?

I want to make sure she knows she can come crying to me...with all of Brent's dirty secrets.

17

W hen I get home Darron is pissed. He takes one look at my get-up and crosses his arms over his chest.

"Have fun tonight?"

"We were out for a drive…" I start.

"We were just doing some undercover work," Shauna says, flitting around the room.

"Let me get you some blood," I tell her, making a beeline for the kitchen. Darron follows me, all scowls and disapproving glances.

"At any point when you were making poor life decisions, did you think of Shauna?" Darron stage whispers at me.

I pour a tall cup of blood. A year ago I would have been grossed out by the fact that Shauna was going to drink it, but now I don't even think about it. I just grab the sugar, add some heaping spoonfuls and give it a good swirl.

"Of course I thought about Shauna!" I whisper yell back. "I couldn't drug her. And she's going batty not being able to sleep. So I asked her if she wanted to come along. She jumped at the chance."

"Of course she did!" Darron doesn't even bother to use his inside voice. "She's Shauna!" He takes the cup of blood away from me and adds a bunch more sugar. "Did you even think about Shit?!"

"I think about shit all the time," I tell him confused.

"Shit. Your puppy. Kitten. Dalmanther. Thing," Darron clarifies. "You didn't crate him before you left. He chewed through my shoe collection. *My shoe collection, Paige*."

"Oh. Shit, shit." I look around for the puppy. "Please tell me that you're not going to be sporting a new Dalmanther coat like some messed up drag version of Cruella De Ville."

"No. But it was close. I put him in your room. I have no idea what he's doing up there. But whatever it is, it serves you right."

We bring the blood out to Shauna who wants to recount our night's adventures for Darron. He's not having it, though, and says he needs some "me time" and heads off to bed.

"Is he mad at us?" Shauna asks, sipping her blood.

"He's mostly mad at me," I assure her. I wanted to apologize and offer to pay for the shoes, but I have zero money to do that. I don't know if Darron will ever forgive me. He calls his wardrobe the 'second love of his life'.

"What's the next step, boss?" Shauna asks.

I tilt my head. "I need to get some sleep."

"Oh, sure. I guess I'll just be here. Awake, for like, ever."

"You did really well tonight," I tell her.

"I made a lot of noise and got stuck in a jar," she says.

"We went in kind of blind. Maybe you can do some research? You can tell me a bit more about the Monarchs. That way next time we'll be prepared."

"We...?" Shauna looks so happy I said we. "I can do that. I have the time."

"Great. Yes." I head up to my room and am happy to find only one of my pillows has been chewed up. But at least Shit is happy to see me and jumps on me, licking my face. I change into my pajamas and snuggle up with him on the bed. His warm little body next to mine makes me forget the destructive force of nature that he is.

Well, mostly forget.

I'm about to fall asleep when I get a text message from Liam.

Still on for tomorrow night?

After a moment of hesitation, I text back a thumbs up. But then that seems a little too unenthusiastic, so I add a happy face with it.

He sends a happy face back. And, *I have an idea, but if it's too cheesy let me know.*

Cheesy? I text back. *I'd be okay with actual cheese. Yummy.*

That can be arranged, he responds. *I was thinking romantic picnic beneath the stars. Spotting constellations and all that rubbish.* He adds a sheepish emoji to the end of this.

For a second my heart skips as I wonder how he knows about the story of how my parents met, but then I realize that of course he's just seen my tattoo and concluded that I'm a star-watching type of girl. Which I'm not. Or at least, no guy that I've been with has ever tried to romance me that way. And if any of them did, I assume they just wanted a chance to feel me up in some random field. But with Liam I already know it won't be like that. He'll be sweet and earnest.

Or maybe happy that he got me in a deserted place to kill me.

I promised McGinnis I'd meet him in a public place. That I'd be careful. But the panic of seeing that picture has receded. Everything in me wants to trust Liam. And I don't think that's my heart—or libido—talking.

The truth is, people are constantly revealing themselves.

I always knew Jax was an incurable flirt with the attention span of a mayfly.

I always knew that Brent was a control freak with something dark glimmering just beneath the layer of his skin.

In both cases, it was what I liked about them.

Maybe Liam doesn't get me as hot and bothered—I mean we spent a whole night just snuggling! I'm more warm and slightly flustered with Liam and I like that. I'd like to be with someone who's an escape from the craziness in the rest of my life.

Not rubbish at all, I type now. *I'll bring a bottle of wine.* I add a wink emoji, letting him make of it what he will.

Predictably, after a slight pause he responds with a blushing emoji and *I can't wait!*

Letting my phone rest in my lap, I realize that I don't need McGinnis to check on Liam. I trust him. And I want to do what any sane adult should've done in the first place—asked him about the creepy pics in his underwear drawer.

It's not too late. I'll do it tomorrow.

I text McGinnis, keeping it short I simply write that Liam and I are good and the mission is off. My phone rings less than a minute later.

"He sweet talked himself into your bed and your good graces?" McGinnis asks in greeting. It is not the tone or the type of style I'm used to hearing from him.

"Excuse me?"

"I said—" His voice is heated, angry, but then he cuts off so suddenly it's almost like our connection is broken. A moment later he sighs. "I'm sorry," he says. It's like another person took the phone, except it still sounds like McGinnis, but this time it's the McGinnis I'm used to. "Forgive me, Paige. I'm worried about you. In my line of work, I've seen a lot of sick shit done to women by men they trust. I don't want that to be you."

"If you want to clean up, you and your department need to raid Super Au Naturel. Harmargan has actual slaves there."

"How do you know what's going on in that vile place?" McGinnis asks.

"It doesn't matter, but it's really messed up what's going on there."

"Look, it's complicated with supe businesses. There's a system."

"Of bribes?" I ask.

"Not all cops are dirty, Paige," he tells me.

"I know that," I say.

"I'll see if I can do something about Au Naturel, but I can't make any promises. That's a big ask. This Liam guy, though...are you sure you don't want me to check him out? He could actually be a bad guy."

"It's fine," I tell McGinnis now. "I appreciate your concern. I just decided that I should have a conversation with Liam before having you break into his house. I mean, if a guy did that to me and I found out about it..." I pause, really thinking about it. Wouldn't it be my luck to realize Liam's a good guy only to lose him because he doesn't trust me? "If he doesn't answer me or his answers don't add up, then we'll go back to the breaking in plan."

McGinnis grumbles a bit but finally gives in, saying, "It's your funeral," before hanging up the phone. It's not quite the same as my dad's "you're a big girl." A little less you get to make your own choices, and a bit more, I can't stop you from being a dumbass.

I sigh and rub Shit's belly, glad that there's at least one man in my life I haven't yet disappointed.

18

I wake up shivering, confused as to how I can be so cold. Heat rises, and my attic bedroom is generally cozy. The pile of shredded cloth at the foot of my bed explains everything.

"Shit!" I yell, and his little spotted head pops up from what's left of my comforter. And sheets. Plus one pillow. Also he seems to have gotten all the way down to the mattress pad at some point during the night. And is that an exposed spring?

"Not cool, Shit. Very bad dog," I say, shaking my finger at him. He hangs his head and looks so forlorn that I immediately open my arms to let him jump into them, which he does...but also sprays me with a little bit of joy urine.

"Okay, that's it—outside!" I say. Miraculously, he hops out of bed and heads downstairs, his tail curled in an adorable little question mark as I follow him to the front room, where he calmly reaches up, pulls down on the latch and lets himself outside. He even closes the door behind him.

"Did you see that?" I ask, spinning to ask Shauna, who

is...actually, what the hell is she doing? It looks like Crafters Gone Wild has met CSI in my living room.

On the wall, where the TV would go if it hadn't been wrecked for the millionth time, is something out of a show, one where the lead detective is a few screws short of a hardware store.

Photos, maps, and papers are taped up everywhere. Some are people and places I recognize, like Charms and Canwella, but others are new to me. There's also various colored string connecting the documents. One runs across the living room to the opposite wall, where there is a picture of me in the center.

Shauna stands there, placing a pink string between me and a picture of Liam. "What is this insanity?" I ask.

Shauna jumps a little, her pixie wings popping out of her back. "Oh, I didn't see you there," she says. She sips a mug of warm blood.

"Do you need a refill?" I ask, jumping on a chance to hide some sugar in her cup.

"No, I just got this one. Though it does taste better when you or Darron make it for me. I wonder why? It must be a mental thing. Like how hot chocolate always tastes better from a cart. I miss hot chocolate. And marshmallows." She takes a wistful sip.

"How are you doing?" I ask, putting aside the manic conspiracy wall for a moment.

"Good. After you went to sleep I got a real rush, actually. Worked on our suspect wall..." She motions to the map and photograph-heavy area. "Then I started to lag, so I got myself some blood. It's not really helping, though. I just want to lay on the couch and watch TV. But there's no TV. So here we are." She shrugs.

"And this?" I ask of the giant picture of me. I'm drinking

a margarita and have a cigarette in my hand. I look drunk AF. She must have snapped it when I wasn't looking. "Where did you even print..."

"I went to your office, used your printer..."

"You took Vanna?" I ask. I'm not opposed to the idea, I just have only one set of keys. She probably talked Vanna into helping her out.

"No, I flew," she tells me. "Your office was locked, though, so I shrunk down and got in through the vent. Then I hacked your computer."

"You what?!"

"Well, I say *hacked,* but your password was really easy to guess. Who uses their own name as their password?"

"It was my dad's, I never changed it," I admit.

"There is no place in cyber security for sentimentality," she tells me.

I blink. Is this down-to-business Shauna? I've never seen her like this. Suddenly I actually believe she was in a committed grown-up relationship and had a real job with FBI-level responsibilities.

"I did most of my pre-research at your office, but I figured you'd want to see what I'd done when you woke up, so I Uber-ed back with all this stuff. I finished up what I had on the Monarch wall, so I started this one." She motions to my giant picture. "This is to help you determine which romantic partner to pick."

I let out an *eep.* "Nico Tralano is on the wall," I tell her.

"He sure is!" she says proudly. "Also Jax, but do you see how I linked him to you with a piece of yellow string? That means it's very unlikely that he's the one for you."

"Well, yeah. I mean, if the yellow string isn't a giveaway you could always consider the fact that we're divorced." I take a step closer, and see something truly alarming. "You did *not* put Brent up there."

"I did. But mostly so I could vandalize his picture." Brent has his eyes scratched out and mustache and beard drawn on his perfect face.

"So this black string means...?"

"Dead to us," she answers, "Literally."

"Not literally," I say automatically, though with no hope of my words getting through. Still, I finish the mini-lesson. "He's still alive so he's figuratively dead to us."

"Whatever. *Literally* whatever." Shauna takes another sip of her blood. Her hands are shaking a bit.

"Let me heat that up for you," I offer, hoping I can sneak in some sugar in the process.

"I'm fine, really," she says. She looks haggard, and there's none of the Shauna spunk that I know and...well, maybe not love. But it's what makes Shauna Shauna. "Should we go over what I learned about the Monarchs? My research starts in the 1850s. That was as far back as I could find."

"This is all great, really," I tell her, "but I have to head to work. Can we go over this when I get home?"

Her entire face falls. "Hey...maybe I can come to your wo—"

Oh no. I got to shut that shit down. "I have a favor to ask you, though," I hastily interrupt.

"You do? What?" she asks eagerly.

"Shit is on Darron's shit list. Could you watch him today? Maybe take him to the park? Keep him out of trouble?"

"I can definitely do that," she assures me.

"Great, he's outside right now, so..." but she's already gone. Ten seconds later she returns with a struggling Shit in her arms.

"We're gonna have so much fun today. Yes we are, yes we are. Who's a good boy?"

"Thank you, Shauna. I do appreciate everything you're doing."

She grins, then takes Shit's paw and has it wave to me. "Say goodbye to mommy." She uses a baby voice to say, "Goodbye mommy!"

"Goodbye weirdos," I tell them. Hopefully Shit and Shauna will keep each other occupied while I'm at work. But in a constructive 'let's play catch' kind of way and not 'let's destroy everything nice in the house' way.

Honestly, with those two, it's a toss up.

19

I stop at the office to make sure Shauna didn't destroy anything while she was here last night.

Oh who am I kidding?

Shauna definitely caused damage, my main goal is to find out how much.

It's worse than I hoped, but better than I expected.

The files that I once spent a long weekend arranging into some used filing cabinets are littered across the floor, almost like Shauna flung them into the air. Getting it all sorted again is gonna suck up another weekend of my time and I'm not thrilled about it. But that's not the thing that really pisses me off.

Shauna raided my mini fridge and totally cleaned out my beer supply. The crazy thing is, she doesn't even like beer. It's way too bitter for her. The six empties scattered across the floor tell me she put it somewhere. If not in her own gut then—

Oh crap.

I catch sight of Vee huddled beneath my desk looking

green. Normally that's a good healthy color for a plant, but this isn't Vee's normal green. She looks waxy rather than lush and her leaves droop pathetically. Beside her is a small pile of what looks and smells like fresh mulch. Did Vee...*puke*?

"Aw, Vee," I say, pulling her out. "Did Shauna get you drunk?"

According to Shauna, Vee once belonged to her wife Tina. The two of them got separated on a mission, long before Tina ghosted. Shauna was shocked to see Vee in my office when she stopped by one day. But it wasn't exactly a happy reunion. As soon as Shauna mentioned Tina's name —Vee attacked. It's been the same ever since. Anytime Shauna comes into my office Vee tries to take a bite out of her.

I'm guessing Shauna watered Vee with my beer supply hoping to mellow her out. And when it worked, Shauna—being Shauna—went overboard and gave Vee all my beer.

I bring Vee over to the window, putting her right into a bright shift of light. Her head swings away, burrowing beneath some leaves. I get it, I also want to hide in the dark when I'm hungover too. But being a plant, I'm hoping the sunshine will help Vee recover faster.

Leaving Vee on the windowsill, I gather the papers covering my floor into a rough pile and put them aside for later. Then I check my messages, crossing my fingers for a paying job. No luck. I do, however, have a message from Officer Esposito.

She tells me we're going clubbing tomorrow night and I need to look hot. She's got her eye on twin Cheetah shifters who she insists are the REAL DEAL. Emphasis hers. The only problem, apparently, is that they will only date other twins. But she thinks with our dark hair and dark eyes we can pass ourselves off as fraternal twins. The message ends with her ordering me to be ready at nine.

I write down the details and figure I'll call her with an excuse to get out of this later today.

Before leaving and heading over to Charms, I pour some water and two ground up ibuprofen into Vee's pot. Giving her head a soft pat, I offer the best words of encouragement I know, "This too shall pass."

Two seconds later I have to remind myself of those words as an angry one-eyed werewolf blocks my office doorway.

Not that Nico is in werewolf form, but when he gets all bristly like this, it's easy to see the animal on the other side of his skin.

"What the fuck, Paige?" he growls. "Do you have a death wish? You went skipping into Au Naturel without me for backup?"

"Who told you that?" I demand. I haven't even told Canwella yet.

"Are you kidding?" Nico rolls his eyes. "It's the best joke going around in the underworld. A pixie and a human brunette with more boob than brain walk into Au Naturel—"

I cut Nico off before he can get any farther. "Just get to the punchline."

Nico's eyes narrow. "Harmargan is the joke. All anyone knows is you somehow got the best of him. That's the punchline. You think he's gonna let that stand?"

I put a hand on his chest, intending to push him out of the way. Nico doesn't budge. Meanwhile, my palm and the pads of my fingers absorb a whole multitude of sensations. Heat. Soft nubby t-shirt. And a hard wall of muscle.

Quickly I snatch my hand back.

"Sorry," I say, trying to sound bored even though my heart is beating a little too fast. "Are we working together now? Because I thought since you'd looked into the Monarchs, it was my turn to—"

Nico cuts me off. "You're pissed that I did my job—the job you brought me in to do—without you? That's why you risked your life?" Well, when he says it like that, it does sound kind of dumb. But I'm not gonna let him twist things around. "I risked my life because this is more than just another job for me. I need Canwella to get her money back, so I can pay my bills this month."

"You could ask me for a loan. You know I'd spot you."

"I don't want a loan," I say, horrified at the idea of being indebted to Nico. "All I want is for you to treat me like an equal. Like we're both equally capable of getting to the bottom of this."

Nico gives me a look that can only be described as condescending. "Paige, we're not equals. I'm a licensed P.I., you're a cleaning lady. In case you haven't noticed, I work alone. So please turn off the little buddy movie you got playing in your head, cause it's not happening. Not today. Not tomorrow. Not ever."

My hands ball into fists, but I know Nico can easily block at punch I throw at him. Usually Nico's macho man thing doesn't bother me...or it only hot and bothers me. But this right here is not sexy in any way. It's clear that Nico needs to be put back into his place.

Drawing myself up to my full height—I give Nico my best death glare. "Canwella is counting on me to get her house back in order," I tell him. "I brought you in as a subcontractor. Which means that technically, you're working beneath me on this job."

Okay, I'm making that up and I'm not sure Canwella

would back me on this. But at least it wipes that smug master of the universe expression off Nico's face. Unfortunately, it's replaced by a flash of anger that makes me feel like I'm standing at the rim of an active volcano. Before I can step back, Nico drags a hand through his hair and when our eyes meet again the tension filling his body has eased and his mouth is quirking upward.

"Working beneath you, huh?" His teeth come out as he grins widely. They're not the yellow fangs I once would've expected but instead perfectly straight pearly whites. "Is that how you want it, Paige?"

There's no missing his meaning. Or that he's changed tactics. Unable to beat me with brute force, he's now turning on the smolder.

I wish I could say that it doesn't work on me. But when his voice dips into that lower and slightly rough register, there's no stopping the warm feeling in my belly.

Nico is no longer blocking my way, he's sort of slid sideways and is now leaning against the wall to my left. It'd be easy to slip around him and drive off.

But there's no way I'm letting him get the last word.

Sticking my nose in the air, I give a slight shake of my head. "I've got to go check-in with Canwella. Once I decide our next move, I'll let you know." Stepping around him, I give him a faux smile. "I know it's hard for big alpha guys like you to take orders from a woman, but it'll get easier over time."

Nico lets me get onto the sidewalk but then grabs my arm right before I step off the curb. I can't see him but I can feel the heat and power of him directly behind me. "You gonna train me like you're training Shit? Sit. Beg. Come."

He leans in with that last word, his breath warm on the back of my neck. I clench all the muscles in my body to keep from visibly shivering, to keep him from knowing how close I am to melting.

Jerking away, I open Vanna's door and slide in. Before closing it behind me, I call over my shoulder, "Try this one. Stay, Nico. Good boy."

I risk one glance back as we're pulling away. But Nico is gone. Of course he didn't stay.

Releasing a shaky breath, I decide that next time I'll just let Nico have the last word and get out before he can turn my insides to jelly.

20

W alking into Charms never ceases to amaze me. The outside looks like any residence on the street—tidy lawn, community-approved mailbox, a hand-painted sign that says HOME resting on the porch. It's when you go inside and are hit by the mix of cigarette smoke, scented candles, and—let's face it—sex, that you realize a suburban soccer mom doesn't live here.

My nose curls a little more than usual, and I count backwards to make sure I didn't miss a cleaning day. There's a scent in the air I can't quite place, and while I'm not exactly "Nico the Nose," I have become fairly adept at identifying the different supe smells. Either Canwella has been doing more business than usual, I over-diluted my cleaner last time, or something is rotten in the state of Denmark.

I smile at my own Shakespeare allusion, pleased that I can mine something out of the expensive English degree sitting on the shelf back in my Down & Dirty office. I'm pulling up my hair when Canwella comes around the corner, clearly upset.

"Oh, Paige!" she cries out, so happy to see me that I'm

immediately enfolded in an ogre hug. Which isn't actually all that unpleasant. They smell like dried flowers and give just the right amount of almost-bone-crushing force. "I'm so glad you're here, hon," she says, wiping away a tear.

I mean, I'm really just here to clean, but apparently I've also become Canwella's shoulder to cry on. Like, a lot. I wish I'd brought an extra shirt.

"Seraphina came back," Canwella tells me. "Only to tell me that she's leaving again!" she wails, throwing her head back and moaning. I can see that she still has her tonsils. Interesting...supes have tonsils. I learn something new every day.

"Leaving?" I repeat. "But Seraphina never goes anywhere...she just sits in her tub all day."

"I know!" Canwella says, pleased to have the backup. "It doesn't make sense. None of this! First the robbery, now Seraphina is leaving and...and..." Her eyes overflow again.

"And Romy and I got into a pretty bad fight this morning," she admits, reaching out to grasp my hand. "I'm so sorry."

"Sorry? Why are you apologizing to me?" I ask.

"Oh...you don't know? When ogres get upset our emotions trigger our sweat glands to release a toxin—"

I hold up my hand, cutting her off. "Is that what I smell?"

"Yes," she confirms, nodding. "It's a defense mechanism that we haven't evolved from yet. I'm sure a long time ago it was helpful to smell repulsive when you charged into the field of battle. But now...well...I can't even tell you how many ogre divorces end with our homes having to be fumigated."

"Okay," I say, digging through my cleaning bucket. "I'm sure I have something here that can take care of it."

"Oh, thank you," Canwella says. "Again, I'm just so sorry.

I caught Romy sneaking in late last night, and she won't tell me where she was. I pried and pried and eventually we both blew our tempers."

"I'm assuming you mean that literally?" I ask with a sigh. I figure the only way to beat back the spread of misuse is to aggressively sprinkle it into my own speech, leading the way by example.

Canwella has the grace to blush. "Yes, actually. In very angry circumstances it's not uncommon for us to...project our feelings."

"As in, *projectile*?" I ask.

"Yes," she nods solemnly. "All over the walls in the kitchen. Sorry about that," she adds, reaching out to pat my arm.

I head into the kitchen to check out the damage, and it's only then that I realize I'll be packing in the extra duty for no pay. The walls are running with something that has the consistency of mucus from a head cold, and about the same color, too. Guess I'm bringing out the big boys today.

I dig into my caddy and pull out my shoulder-length rubber gloves...and a windshield scraper. I learned a long time ago that supernatural cleaning often means being inventive with everyday objects.

While I work I let my mind wander—being here both physically and mentally is not an option. My first priority needs to be figuring out who robbed Charms so that I can get Canwella's money back— and get paid. But my mind wants to linger on more pleasant things, like my date with Liam tonight. Talking to Brent on the phone at Au Naturel only reinforced how wonderful Liam is, what a nice guy. A nice, normal guy.

I mean, sure he has that murderous father thing. But it's like a scar on a super-hot guy—it just assures you that no one is perfect. Yep, Liam is definitely a step up. A whole flight of stairs up.

I'm scraping the last of the ogre tantrum off a sticky spot on the stove when something shiny catches my eye. I pluck it from the congealing goo and hold it up to the light, recognizing a scale. I've seen plenty of these in Seraphina's *Splash* room, but hers are iridescent, changing colors in the light from a pearly pink to a muted blue. This scale is grayish, with flecks of brown.

Just then I hear an argument breaking out. It's not an unusual occurrence. Even though Charms is an upscale place, there is the occasional customer who wants something a little more in the line of what Au Naturel offers— and Canwella firmly shuts them down and tosses them out. But it's not a customer that the ogre madame is arguing with. It's Seraphina—and she's yelling.

I hurry down the hall to find Canwella standing in the *Splash* doorway, her arms on either side, her skin turning a mottled shade as she shouts.

"You don't know what you're doing!" Canwella cries. "You're like a daughter to me. I can't just let you wander out into—"

"A daughter? Ha!" Seraphina yells, as she stuffs handfuls of clothing into a suitcase. "That's funny, considering you don't even know what Romy is up to! Or should I say, who's up in her?"

"You fishy little...." Canwella goes a new shade of red, and I'm worried she's about to blow her temper all over the hallways. I just stripped off my shoulder-length yellow rubber gloves; I'm not doing that again.

"Okay, time out, everyone calm down," I say, interceding. "Why don't you come sit down in the nice, clean kitchen and have a drink?" I put my hands on Canwella's shoulders and steer her down the hall, ready to duck if she blows a valve.

I get her settled at the table with a tall gin and head back to Seraphina's room. The mermaid's case is packed, but she's sitting in her tub, fin hanging out the side, tears streaming down her cheeks.

"I love this room, all the water features, I'm going to miss it," she admits, her face screwing up in agony.

I sigh and flop into one of the overstuffed chairs. This isn't the first time I've been on the receiving end of a Charms-confession. The residents like to dish, and I have to admit I've learned a thing or two from them...maybe some things I can try on Liam tonight?

"Then why leave?" I ask. "You can see how upset Canwella is. She doesn't want you to go."

"Of course she doesn't," Seraphina cries, flicking her fin and sending some water in my direction. "I make her a lot of money."

"You're more than just a dollar sign to Canwella," I tell her. "She cares about all of you. Believe me, I've been in establishments where the owners don't care about their workers. You've got it good."

Seraphina sighs, twirling her hair. "You're right... but maybe it's too good, you know? I never wanted to leave this place. I was happy to sit in my tub and do my work and never let the outside world in. But what kind of a life is that?"

I can kind of relate. I've been letting the outside world—supes—in for a while now. And it has made my life decidedly messy, but also a lot more interesting.

"Did you meet someone?" I pry, hoping to learn something positive that maybe will assuage Canwella's nerves. If Seraphina is leaving with a loyal customer, maybe the madame can come around to the fact, feel more like a matchmaker.

"Oh, no!" Seraphina says with a laugh. "Not here! But, I guess in a way, yes. I have met a group of people. And they helped me. I've seen a bigger world now, and I want to be a part of it. They made me see that there's more than life between these four walls. Or—well, this tub, anyway," she says, smacking the sides.

She looks happy, but her words are setting off alarm bells in my head. *They? Group?* Does this have to do with that podcast Canwella was talking about—Together We Come? She'd been worried that Seraphina was buying into their concept—that supes and humans should just overcome their differences by "fucking it out," more or less. I make a mental note to check out an episode when I have some time. It doesn't sound like a good thing for a nice girl like Seraphina to get involved in.

"What do you mean?" I press. "Who are you talking about? How did you meet them?"

"It doesn't matter," Seraphina says airily, pulling the plug on her tub and shifting back into a human, her perfectly shaped legs now dangling over the side of the tub. She gets out, water running down her naked body as she swipes at herself with a towel, then seems to realize she put every last stitch of clothing she owns into the suitcase. Irritated, she pops it open, yanking out a pair of sweatpants and a hoodie.

"At least leave some contact information?" I plead. "Something so that Canwella can get a hold of you. I know you want to go, but she's worried about you."

Seraphina pulls her wet hair out of the back of her hoodie, and yanks her phone from where it had been resting on the side of the tub. She asks for my number, then sends me her contact info.

"You can share that with Canwella," she says. "But please give me a few days to get settled into my new life, okay?"

I nod. I don't know exactly what I'm agreeing to, but there's not a whole lot I can do. I don't think I can argue with her when I don't even know what I'm up against. I slip my phone back into my pants pocket and my fingers brush against something.

"Oh hey," I say, plucking the scale from my pocket. "I found this in the kitchen when I was cleaning up after Canwella and Romy. I didn't think it was yours, but I wasn't sure."

Seraphina takes one glance at it, her mouth going into a thin line as she snaps her suitcase shut again.

"It's not mine," she says stiffly, heading for the door. "And it's not really my business. Charms is my past." She takes a deep breath, as if she's concentrating. Then closes her eyes. "In order to access my best future, I have to make the right decisions in my present, which will leave my questionable past behind me." She says it like she's quoting someone. Or as if it's some sort of mantra.

"What about your friends here?" I ask, worried for her. Cutting people off from everyone and everything they love leads to control and abuse.

"They weren't my friends, they were only holding me back," she says it sadly, but wholeheartedly. I'm getting the bad idea she's been brainwashed, but before I can ask more questions, she's out the door.

"Paige," she turns back at the top of the stairs. Her eyes shift back to the scale resting in my hand. "There's lot of snakes out there. Be careful."

21

———

At home, Shauna is sitting on the couch, curled up with Shit. Shit tries to squirm away but Shauna grabs him back and wraps him up in a blanket, like she's swaddling a baby. Darron sits on the couch and they're all mindlessly starting at the TV.

Wait...a TV?

"Where did this come from?" I ask.

"Jax dropped it off. He moved in with Kimmy, so they had lots of extra stuff."

"They LOVED the decorations. CSI chic?" Darron snipes.

"Oh. Right." I sit next to Shauna and let Shit lick my face.

The last time Jax lived with a woman—it was me. A heaviness pools in my heart. Not just because I once loved Jax and thought we'd be together forever. But also because moving in with your girlfriend is so normal and healthy and adult. Meanwhile, I'm living with a pixie, a Dalmanther, and a drag queen. How did my screw-up of an ex become more stable than me?

"And what have you been up to today?" I ask, trying to distract myself from these depressing thoughts.

"We played, then played some more." Shauna looks at me, dark circles under her eyes. "Are there more hours in the day than there used to be?" she asks.

"Still twenty-four," Darron assures her.

"It seems like more. I'm just so tired, but I can't sleep." She hugs Shit to her chest.

"Do you want to talk me through what you found out about the Monarchs?" I ask. She shrugs.

Darron catches my eye and I follow him into the kitchen. "I am so sorry about your shoe collection," I start.

He shrugs. "It's not as bad as I first thought, though I have been repairing puncture marks all day. A few are not salvageable."

"I will make it right," I tell him.

He offers me a small smile. "Shit happens," he says.

I laugh. "That's my life motto."

I know it's not all better between us, but it's a start. "Hey, what's up with Shauna?" I ask.

"Oh, you mean that gooey pile of despair on the couch? By my count she's been really and truly sugar-free for"— Darron quickly counts on his fingers— "twenty hours? All last night and this morning she was making her own blood—"

"With no idea that we've been secretly spiking it," I interrupt.

"Exactly. I tried to make her a cup with just a little bit of artificial sweetener in. I thought maybe we could help wean her off that way, but she wouldn't even drink it."

"Probably for the best," I say. "That fake stuff will kill you."

Darron gives me a deadpan look. "She's already dead, remember?"

"Right," I say. It's funny, but I actually forget sometimes. Except for drinking blood, Shauna doesn't act very vampire-y. Probably all the beauty she was doing.

"Anyway, I don't think sugar is the problem at this point," Darron adds. "She says she's not hungry. She's just despondent."

"She's actually going through withdrawal now," I tell him. "Shit!" There's a small bark from the other room.

"She hasn't moved off the couch for hours," he tells me. "Maybe she just needs to wait it out?"

I nod. "I don't want to seem like a selfish bitch…"

"Too late," Darron tells me, but his voice is joking. Mostly.

"Hilarious. The thing is, I have a date with Liam tonight."

He rolls his eyes.

"What? You don't like Liam?"

"I don't know Liam. He seems fine, a bit vanilla, sure. But you have that beefcake of a werewolf sniffing after you and you're going on an actual date with Liam. Is it to make Nico jealous?"

"I am NOT trying to make anybody jealous," I tell him.

"Then it's the accent?"

"No! Liam's not as boring as you think!" I tell him. I fill him in on what's going on, and he listens intently.

"Let me get this straight…" he recaps. "Liam's dad was some kind of British supe-killing Ted Bundy. Dear old Liam fled to America to make a new life, but he may or may not be the vampire serial killer that has been stalking you?" He crosses his arms. "And now your crazy ass is going on a date with him to some very private spot to watch the stars or possibly get murdered?"

"That's all about right. Except the last bit. He won't murder me. I'm, like, ninety-eight percent sure on that."

"Right. But in the instance of that two percent chance that you don't come home?"

"Call McGinnis. Nico too. Like just scream until there's a full search party."

He shakes his head. "Girl, how does all this drama find you?"

"I wish I knew."

"I think this is a bad idea. Why don't you just have dinner in a well-lit restaurant and do the stargazing another night?"

It's a good question. And it's not like I haven't thought of texting Liam to change our plans. But every time I talk myself out of it.

The truth is, I need to believe in Liam. But even more...I need to believe in myself. I gotta prove that I'm not just a magnet for messed-up men. Because if I am then I need to invest in a whole collection of high-end vibrators and forget about ever having a healthy relationship. If I can't tell the difference between a sweet guy and a totally psychopathic killer, then I am broken in a major way.

And I don't want to be broken. Or alone forever.

I want what Darron had with his wife. What Shauna had with Tina.

I want a relationship that doesn't end with me asking myself, "Dear God what was I thinking?"

But I'm not gonna go into all that with Darron. Keeping it short and sweet, I simply say, "I think I'm safe. And even if I were in danger, I can handle myself."

"I'm not going to talk you out of this, am I?" he asks.

"Nope. McGinnis couldn't either."

"Well, let's pick out your outfit. What says, 'Don't murder me', these days?"

"I was thinking of jean shorts and a tube top," I mostly say because I know it will upset him.

"Look, Daisy Duke, I am not letting you get murdered in your white trash work clothes." He takes me by the arm and leads me through the living room to his back bedroom. "Shauna!" he calls. "I'm going to play dress up with Paige, wanna come?"

"Nah," Shauna says, raising a hand. "Too tired. Aaaaand..." she raises her arm slightly, "TV."

Darron pulls me into his room and opens his closet doors. "Let's get you dressed for your date with VSK!"

22

I'm still feeling gun-shy after shooting that vamp the other day. My gun feels too heavy in my hands as I check that it's loaded, click the safety on, and then tuck it into the back waistband of my pants.

"Not really how I would've accessorized that outfit," Darron says as he observes my final date preparations. "But considering the circumstances, I approve."

Trying to make light of it, I force a smile. "Maybe someday when I'm not broke, I'll upgrade to something with a pearl handle. That way I'll have a gun that works better with evening wear."

"Pearl handle?" Darron gives me a pitying look and shakes his head. "Oh honey...no. That's for old ladies. Just stick with basic black."

"I might be an old lady by the time I'm not broke," I say, hoping it doesn't end up being true.

"True," Darron agrees. "Maybe if you're going to risk your life for a date it should be with a man who has a better job. As a tour guide I don't think your Liam is going to be able to give you a life of luxury."

"I don't need a life of luxury," I shoot back at Darron. "I need a life of normalcy. And that's what Liam would be."

"Except for his Daddy issues," Darron is quick to point out.

I sigh. Yeah, except for that.

"There's still time to text him and make an excuse," Darron says as I check my hair one more time. "Headache. Cramps. The painful realization that this date is a terrible idea?"

I turn to face Darron head on. "When I found out Jax was cheating on me, I was so mad. Not just at him. I was lashing out at everyone. My parents included. One day I said to my dad, 'How could you let me marry him? Why didn't you stop me?'"

In my mind I can see the moment so clearly. It was fall and I was helping him rake leaves. It was a cold day, and my dad was wearing gloves and a hat. But my anger was burning me up from the inside out. Even though my fingers were blue with cold, I couldn't feel it.

"What did he say?" Darron asks, his voice gentle.

"He said that everyone—me included—knew that Jax wasn't the safest bet. But love was an act of bravery." I smile, even though my throat grows thick as I remember the rumble of dad's voice. "Then he added, 'and stupidity too.'" I laugh. "My mom came out around then. Her and dad started on this whole bit about how they'd raised me to be brave and stupid, not scared and smart."

"Well, that does clock with what I know of you," Darron says. His voice is wry but his gaze as it falls on me is warm. He opens his arms and I fall into them. We share a quick hard squeeze of a hug. I know he's thinking of his wife who ghosted while I'm remembering my parents. Sometimes it feels like all of us who lost someone in the Great Ghosting will never truly be whole again.

The doorbell rings just as Darron and I pull apart.

"There's your man," Darron says. "Go be the bravest and most stupid you've ever been. Make your parents proud."

———

Liam brings a dog toy for Shit. It looks like a tire wrapped in snow chains.

"Don't worry," He assures me. "It's Dalmanther-safe. I went to three different pet stores just to be sure. This"—he pats the giant tire—"is guaranteed to last for at least one week. Perhaps longer depending on your Dalmanther's destructive drive."

I look at Shit whose eyes are fastened on the tire, like he knows it's for him. "I'd say his destructive drive is ramped to maximum, judging by how much stuff he's already destroyed."

I give the tire a little push, letting it roll down the drive-way. Immediately, Shit takes off after it. His jaw closes around one of the chains and he begins to drag the tire under some bushes near the side of the house.

"Thank you," I say to Liam. "That was very thoughtful, if this keeps him busy for even a few days it'll be a huge relief."

He grins, like my thanks is the best gift of all. "I'm so glad you like it."

Leaning in, I give him a kiss on the cheek. The butter-flies that had filled my stomach dissipate. When Liam isn't in front of me it's easy to imagine he might be VSK. But when he's standing in front of me, smiling in that sheepish way, it's easy to trust him.

"Let's go," I say. And then, because I'm not a complete

idiot, I add, "I'll drive." I point to Vanna. In case my gut is wrong, I'll at least have Vanna for backup.

"Perfect!" Liam easily agrees. "Let me just grab the picnic supplies from the boot of my car."

Once in Vanna, Liam gives her directions to a park I've been to a few times—although not recently. When I was in high school it was a popular make-out spot. That was a long time ago, though. During the early emergence of supes, it became no man's land in a turf war between the fae and vampires. Even though most of those groups have long since broken up, the park never recovered its reputation.

Liam, though, assures me it's perfectly safe. Except for the broken glass from beer and wine bottles. He went earlier in the day and cleared out a spot for us. "I used a battery-powered hand vac on the grass," he admits with a blush. "As a professional, I wasn't sure if you'd approve or be appalled."

With a laugh, I tell him that I love his ingenuity. And I do. It's so sweet of him to make sure that everything is perfect. Even going so far as to vacuum over grass!

I ignore the little voice in my head whispering that maybe it's not sweet. Maybe he was simply staking out the place where I'm going to die. Maybe he also found the perfect place to bury me.

I cut off these thoughts. Or try to. But they won't go away. By the time we reach the park, I realize that I won't be able to enjoy one second of this date until I get the answers I need from Liam.

I watch as he lays out the picnic blanket and then places a huge cooler beside it.

"Liam, I need to ask you—" just as I start to speak, he pipes up too.

"Paige, before we go any further—"

We both stop and do that thing where we say, "You go

ahead," "No you," "No really, you," until finally Liam says, "If you don't mind, I'd rather get this off my chest."

I nod. Instead of speaking, though, he paces a bit like he's trying to get his nerve up again. Finally, he faces me.

"My last serious girlfriend was two years ago. I tried to hide who I was from her. I did hide it quite successfully for nearly a year. Then she found out and…" Liam sighs. "We were done. She couldn't accept it. The truth. But also my lies by omission." He gazes at me with soulful eyes, while my heart beats through my chest. I honestly can't tell if this is him confessing he's VSK or not.

And if he is… shit? What do I do if he is? Because part of me wants to fold him into my arms right now and tell him everything is fine, and we'll get through it together. Another part wants to run, and yet a third part wants to know what the hell TomTom Petty—my neighbor's cat—did to deserve such a grisly death.

"I don't want to make that mistake again," Liam goes on. "I don't want to fall for you and I'm afraid that I already am…" Stopping, he scrubs his hands through his hair. "Bollocks. I'm making a mess of this."

"It's fine," I say, although really I want to scream, SPIT IT OUT! But first I gotta know, "Your ex-girlfriend, what happened to her? Is she, uh…in a better place now?"

Liam grimaces. "I have no idea. You know how it is. We had a huge row. Both said things we shouldn't have. In the end, I had to remove all traces of her from my life. Just move on and never look back."

"Oh. Right," I say, backing up so that Vanna's close by. Liam either just confessed to killing his ex or simply giving all her stuff back.

"Paige, I'll understand if you can't accept this part of me."

"Okay." Three steps closer to Vanna.

"I know you've dealt with a lot already in your life and this might be a bridge too far."

"Okay." Five steps closer.

"But whatever happens, I want you to know the time we've spent together—"

"JUST SAY IT ALREADY!" The words burst out of me as the tension reaches the point of no return. Vanna gives a long-sustained beep after my words as if to weigh in with her agreement.

Liam blushes bright red right up to the roots of his hair. And then blurts out, "My father is a serial killer."

The silence in the park is deafening.

23

"Whaaaaaaat?" I try to fake some surprise, so that he doesn't know I was digging around in his drawers. But first I need to make sure that's all of it. "And..."

"And..." Liam stares at me, clearly unsure of what I'm asking. "I'm his son. Blood of his blood. Shared genes. The apple from his tree and all that."

I release a breath, my bones suddenly wobbly. I mean, sure, this doesn't exonerate him, but would he confess to this if he was VSK?

"Why don't you tell me the whole story?" I say, lowering myself to the blanket, I reach for the cooler. As I hoped, there's both beer and a bottle of wine snuggled in ice at the bottom. I pull out two beers.

He takes it, his look a mixture of hope and uncertainty. "You don't want to leave right now? And never see me again?"

"I want to hear you out. So long as the story doesn't end with you deciding to follow in your father's footsteps."

"It doesn't!" Liam exclaims, eyes wide. "Dear God, quite

the contrary. In no way shape or form do I wish to emulate that man. Growing up he was my hero, of course. I thought he was a good dad. He didn't drink too much. He had a good steady job as a delivery man. And he was good to my mum."

He sits down next to me and I hand him a beer. "In retrospect, he was, well, a bit of a loudmouth. Rather racist as well. As I was growing up our neighborhood became more mixed, immigrants and what-not. He called them all terrorists. It was embarrassing at times, but mostly I just thought, that's my dad. But then the supes came out…" Liam stops and takes a long swig of beer. "He didn't like them from the get-go. No one did, though. I'm sure it was the same here. Everyone was terrified. It was like waking up into a nightmare."

I do remember. The power was not reliable in those days, but Mom, Dad, and I sat in front of the TV even when it wasn't working, just waiting and hoping for more news of what was happening. Then when it finally came on, we'd watch tape of humans shifting into tigers or moving with a speed that seemed impossible but that we'd later learn was normal for vampires. The three of us would shake our heads and say it couldn't be true. Then we'd go and double-check that all the doors were locked.

"They say now," Liam continues, "that the thing that set Dad off was having his truck stolen. That's when he first went out looking for blood. And he found it. My mum and I had no idea. He told us he was out scavenging, trying to make sure we were taken care of. We believed him. Eventually I asked to go with him. I was twenty, too old to be cowering while my father took all the risks. At first he didn't want to bring me along. I thought he wanted to protect me, but now I think he knew I didn't have the stomach for it."

"Maybe both," I offer.

Liam grimaces. "No. He always said I was soft. I went to a private school on scholarship and he always rather looked down on it. Or me. Like I'd betrayed him and our working man roots."

I reach out and touch Liam's shoulder. "He sounds like an arsehole," I say, offering the Brit version in an attempt to get a smile out of him.

It works. Though the smile wavers quickly and then disappears entirely. "Yes, he was. Still, it was a shock when he took me out...hunting supes. At first, I pretended to go along with it. I'm ashamed to admit that, but it's the truth." Liam's voice grows thick. "At one point I actually high-fived him after he shot a vampire point blank right between the eyes. I was in shock, I think. But also trying to justify it, telling myself he just wanted to protect normal people." Liam sighs heavily. "And then we finished in his trophy room. That's where we washed up before going home to Mum. He threatened to kill me if breathed a word of it to her. No," Liam corrects himself. "He didn't threaten. He promised. And by then I'd seen what he was capable of. I knew he'd follow through."

"Oh, Liam," I say.

"I knew Mum and I had to get away. And somehow report him to the authorities as well. I just didn't know how. Things were still so lawless then."

I scooch closer to Liam and take his hand. Even with him beside me, I can feel how scary it must've been. It's amazing he made it through to this moment beside me on a picnic blanket.

"I ended up telling my mum. My plan was to have her slip something into his food to knock him out so we could get away. Once we were safe, I'd get a note to the authorities with the location of his trophy room."

"But?" I ask, because the way he's telling this tells me that things did not go according to plan.

"My mum warned him. I should've seen it coming, she'd kept saying, "This isn't the man I married." I thought she meant it as he was a monster. But she meant it more like, I don't know, she thought he was having some sort of mental breakdown and needed help. She thought if she told him it was wrong, that he'd just...stop."

"Oh wow," I give his hand a hard squeeze, reminding him I'm here and on his side. "I'm guessing he didn't?"

Liam shakes his head. "Ah, no. He led a vampire gang to our house. They knew who he was, and had been casing our home for a while. He knew they were onto him--and he left the doors unlocked one night after he left. Let them in. Let them torture us. They thought they were getting revenge on him, but really he planned it that way. He wanted us to hate them the way he did."

"Liam," I say. I can't get any other words out. The way he says this last bit is so flat and emotionless. I can tell he's bottled it away deeply, that actually allowing himself to remember that moment and be back in it—would be more than he can handle.

Liam releases a long shuddering breath and turns to me with a wan smile, himself once more. "As luck would have it, my father was captured on our third day of captivity. It seems the authorities were onto him as well, and supes have more rights in the UK than they do over here. Dad traded the information that Mum and I were tied up at home, suffering, in order to spare himself the death penalty. So we were saved and he's in prison, and"—Liam swallows hard —"we all lived happily ever after."

"But you work with vampires. How do you not hate them?"

"I don't hate them, not at all. I feel bad for them. Most of them, the ones recently turned, were just normal people. Then wham, they get bitten and turned against their will, then they're just this new thing that's hungry all the time. Can you imagine, suddenly needing to drink a person's blood just to survive? I would hate that to happen to me. I'd never want to live that way. The ones that came to our house, some were newly turned. I could see it in their eyes. They were disgusted with themselves."

"A few…what about the other ones?"

He shrugs. "The other ones weren't even human at all anymore. They'd lost themselves completely." He shivers.

I know there's more to the story. The aftermath of his father's capture must've been hell, enough to drive Liam overseas to a new life in a foreign country. But I don't need those details. Not tonight. Not when the stars are appearing overhead.

I kiss him with as much tenderness as I can muster. He kisses me back and what started out sweet, quickly grows hotter. Clearly, my old high school make-out spot still has that old magic, because before I know it, I'm helping Liam pull my shirt off.

"Paige," he gasps as I work the button on his jeans. "I didn't tell you that story to get into your pants. Or er, to get you into mine."

"I know," I tell him, as I finally jerk the button free. "You didn't have to. I've been wanting to get naked with you for a while."

"Oh goodness, me too," Liam says, his voice thin as my hand slides down into his pants. "I wanted you so badly the other night. But not before you knew about my dad. And you were in such a bad place after shoo—hhhhhhaaaaa." As my hand closes around Liam's cock, he finally runs out of words.

Well, almost.

"Paige," he exclaims and then he's on top of me, pushing my own pants down. Beneath me, my gun presses into my lower back and I feel like a bit of an idiot for bringing it. As Liam pulls a condom out of his wallet (apparently some habits are trans-atlantic) I slither sideways, so the gun is no longer digging directly into my backbone.

"C'mon," I say to Liam, as he gets the condom into place, the darkness from earlier not gone, but simply packed away. Amazingly, it makes me like Liam more. He's not the perfect guy—and that's a relief. I would never fit with someone like that. Instead he's perfectly imperfect. "Let's shag already."

He looks down at me with twinkling eyes. "Usually when we Brits talk about shags, it's in terms of having a quick one."

"Is that what we're gonna do?"

He grins. "Not if I can help it."

While we don't break any world records for time spent doing the horizontal mambo (and really who would want— the chafing!), our first time together in no way comes close to qualifying as a quick shag.

We snuggle beneath the stars and eat cheese and crackers and strawberries. I point out Ursa Minor and Ursa Major and then tell Liam the story of how my parents met. He tells me how close he is with his mom, and that she was so sorry about betraying him to his father but in the end it brought them closer together.

"I'd love to meet her someday," I say, assuming she's in England and that day is far off.

But to my surprise, Liam says, "How about next weekend? I'm meeting her for our monthly lunch."

"That's a long flight for just lunch," I joke, stalling.

"She moved across the pond with me, though she settled in the country. Her garden is amazing. I never have to buy veg with all she gives to me."

"Cool," I say, trying to hide my discomfort with the idea of putting this relationship into a higher gear. The highest gear, really. Meeting parents is major. And although I like Liam, I don't think we're quite there yet. To make things worse, I've just realized that the mosquitoes have come out and are eating us alive. I start slapping at them. "Maybe we should get dressed," I say.

"Right." Liam grabs my clothes for me, before reaching for his own. Quickly, we dress, gather the picnic stuff, and climb back into Vanna.

"This has been fun," I start to say as the engine turns.

Liam interrupts me. "Paige, I didn't mean to make things weird. You don't have to meet my mum. Or you can, but it doesn't have to be MEETING MY MUM." He pauses, and then smiles bashfully. "Although, it also could be that, er, the ya know, meeting my mum as my girlfriend. Official, like we're going steady as a pair, Friendbook official and what-not." He stammers a bit and runs his hands through his hair, in his adorkable Brit way. "Or not, if I'm moving too fast. I know this night has been, a lot. It's just...I really really like you, Paige."

Oh wow. He doesn't just like me. He really *really* likes me. And wants to make it Friendbook official.

And I'm glad we're having the conversation. It's always awkward getting to that point in a relationship where you want to make sure you're both on the same page. I'm usually the first to broach it. At my age, the idea of 'going steady' or even being someone's 'girlfriend' sets my teeth on edge a bit.

So I usually keep things simple. "I'm fucking only you. Are you fucking only me?"

But I know Liam is asking for more. He opened up to me. I know his whole history. We had romantic picnic blanket sex. He wants more than just exclusive banging rights. I can feel him slowly edging up to the L word.

And...I'm not there yet.

I fall in lust very easily. But love...that's a lot harder. It's totally possible it's all tied up into my trust issues, what with Jax being a cheater and all. He was the first guy I really loved...and I learned that love doesn't always end well.

"I like you too," I say at last. "And I'm, you know, not with anyone else right now." I pause, trying to think of a nice way to say that it's way too soon for me to meet his mom.

But then, I'm saved.

My cellphone rings. And it's Canwella.

"I gotta take this," I tell Liam, truthfully.

"Paige! It's Romy!" Canwella shrieks. Although even her shriek is oddly melodic.

"Another fight?" I ask, trying to suppress a groan as I think about the cleanup on that.

But Canwella quickly changes the direction of my thoughts, "No, not a fight! Romy's gone! She's been kidnapped!"

24

"**K**idnapped?!" I ask. "Was there a note? How do you know?"

After Canwella specifies that there was no note, and that the only indication Romy was kidnapped is that she's no longer at Charms, I breathe a sigh of relief.

Canwella has burrowed her way into my heart, there's no doubt about it. But Romy was unhappy, anyone could see it. Combined with Canwella's high emotional state, I'm fairly certain that she's overreacting.

And I just had first-time sex with Liam. It was kind of perfect, and I don't feel like the follow-up to that should be letting Canwella *project* her feelings all over me. Besides, my cleaning supplies are leaning towards the light side, what with not being able to pay my bills. The shelves in the back of Vanna are decidedly low on bleach and that's something I'll definitely need to clean up after a Canwella blow out.

Instead, I'm firm with her on the phone, insisting that I won't be coming over, but that I'll call her back once I'm "out of my business meeting." Liam covers his mouth at that, and I realize I just exhibited a propensity for casual lying right in front of my new boyfriend and maybe that wasn't very smart. But he seems to be smiling under his hand, so I let it go.

I drop him off and spend a few minutes leaning against the side of his car, nuzzling my face into his neck and letting my hands wander while he moans.

The truth is, I could be up for a round two...and judging by the bulge in his pants, he is, as well. But Vanna issues a series of sharp honks and I pull back.

"Sorry," I tell Liam. "I really do need to return that phone call."

"No problem," he says, bringing me in again for one more kiss. His hand wanders up to my hair and comes back with a twig, which he bops me on the nose with. "Would it be really dorky to keep this as a memory of tonight?"

I laugh, and it's easy. With Brent sometimes I laughed because I thought I was supposed to. With Jax it was always laced with frustration because I knew he was getting away with something. And with Nico I laugh in order to change the subject and not end up naked in his lap. With Liam, I just laugh. And it's a nice, light, carefree sound. Being with Liam is less exciting than those other relationships, but it's a hell of a lot easier. And I could do with a bit more easy in my life.

Liam kisses me one more time, before getting into his car and driving away.

I wait until his taillights fade away, before pulling out my phone to call Canwella back.

"Paige?!" she shrieks into the phone, her opera voice cracking. "We've got to find my little girl! Who knows what they could be doing to her right now?"

I don't bother reminding Canwella that as an ogre, Romy is hardly little. And it's exactly that thought that leads me to my next one. I can't see any species getting the upper hand on an ogre...and I remember the light build of the guy who used the stun gun on me when Charms was robbed. If that crew came back for more, he certainly didn't make Romy do anything she didn't want to.

"Why do you think she's been kidnapped?" I ask. "How do you know she didn't just run away? You guys haven't exactly been getting along lately."

"After you asked about a note, I found one," Canwella says, her voice suddenly less hysterical.

"Oh." There goes my theory about ogres as immovable objects. I really hope I didn't blow off Canwella when Romy is actually in trouble. "What does it say?"

Canwella clears her throat as Vanna pulls into our driveway. The shredded remains of the tire Liam had brought Shit lay in the side yard, reduced to pieces the size of my fingernail.

"It says," Canwella goes on, "You haven't paid. You're going to."

I wait for more as I flick off Vanna's headlights and give her steering wheel a pat. "Is that it?"

"Yes, but don't you see?" Canwella pushes. "It's my bribes! I haven't paid them, and they took Romy! They're going to take it out on her skin!"

"Well, technically if they were going to do that it should read, 'You haven't paid. Now *she's* going to,'" I say.

"Could you not be an English major right now?" Canwella wails, as I walk up to the porch. Shit comes out from under a bush, the chain from his tire wrapped decoratively around him.

"Sorry," I apologize quickly to the ogre madame, going down on one knee to give Shit a rub. He buries his head in my crotch, pulls back, and gives me a side eye.

"Mommy got laid," I tell him in a whisper, and he snorts at me.

"What?" Canwella asks.

"Nothing," I say quickly, pushing open the front door. Shit runs in ahead of me, jumping onto the couch and jerking Shauna out of a deep sleep. She accidentally kicks over a full mug of blood and it goes flying across the papers on the floor she'd apparently been studying before going comatose.

"Shit, you little shit!" Shauna screams, wiping sleep from her eyes.

"What's going on over there?" Canwella asks.

"Normal stuff," I tell her, heading for the stairs and my attic bedroom. "Look," I say, shutting the door behind me after Shit slips in, a bloodied handprint on his ass from where Shauna apparently gave him a smack.

"I don't see that there's a connection between the note and Romy disappearing."

"What?" Canwella asks. "Why not?"

"Think about it," I say, stripping down. Shit steals my underwear and crawls under the bed. I debate crawling after him—it's my good date underwear. But Canwella is gonna lose it if I don't give her my full attention, so I decide to write the underwear off at a loss. Next time we have sex Liam's gonna see the real me—period-stained underwear and everything.

"If someone kidnapped your daughter there would be instructions. Meet me here. Have this much money. Do you want her back alive? *Et cetera.*"

"Uh-huh…" Canwella says, voice hopeful, but not convinced.

"But that's not what happened," I go on. "You got a note from the people you bribe. It only seems threatening because you found it at the same time you realized Romy was gone. All it says is that you're going to pay. I don't think it's anything other than that—a statement that you're overdue and you will pay up."

"But what about Romy?" Canwella wails, the little bit of calm I'd managed to instill evaporating. I imagine paintball-size splatters of her panic on the kitchen ceiling over at Charms.

"Like I said, you two haven't exactly been getting along," I say. Then I remember Seraphina's words to Canwella as she'd been making her exit from Charms, after Canwella had told her she was like a daughter.

You don't even know what Romy is up to! Or should I say, who's up in her?

"Does Romy have a boyfriend?" I ask, suddenly.

"Of course not! She's not allowed to date!" Canwella says, and I have to roll my eyes. Of course the supe madame would have very strict rules for her own daughter. But it's late, and I decide not to point out the hypocrisy. I burrow under my covers just as Shit hops in beside me, nuzzling for warmth.

"I don't think Romy is in any danger," I say, trying to share some of the comfort I feel right now with Canwella. "I truly don't. If I did I'd be over there, trying to figure this out."

"Okay," Canwella says, somewhat mollified. "But what *are* you going to do?"

It's a good question. We've hit a lot of dead ends. Super Au Naturel didn't yield anything other than a series of bad nightmares and the beginning of an ulcer. I don't think the bribe crew sounds like a real threat—they just want their money. And as for money—whoever robbed Charms also hit the Monarch Club, but that hadn't turned up any leads when Nico went there.

A smile spreads across my face, big and confident.

"Nico didn't find anything at the Monarch Club," I tell Canwella, "but that doesn't mean I won't."

"Do you really think you can sniff out something Nico can't?" She sounds dubious, and my smile shrinks.

"It's the difference between being a man or a woman," I say. "Maybe I can get the bartender to talk."

"Oh no," Canwella contradicts me. "You can't walk up in there all slutty. They won't let you through the door."

"What do you mean all slutty?" I ask, my smile totally gone now.

"There's a very strict dress code at the Monarch Club," Canwella tells me. "You can't wear what you'd usually wear."

"Like a general *you*, as in the whole population?" I ask, my voice a little tight. "Or more like *you*, Paige Harper, dress like a slut normally?"

"You're being an English major again," Canwella says. "Listen, all I'm saying is that the Monarch Club isn't Super Au Naturel, and it's not Charms, either. This is a classy joint."

"Black tie only?" I jibe.

"Bow tie," she comes back. There's silence for a second as I try to figure out if she's joking.

"No, really," Canwella goes on. "You have to wear a bow tie."

I grab my laptop off the nightstand and do a quick search on the Monarch Club. Sure enough, there's a posted dress code, and it looks like I'm going to have to raid Darron's closet again.

I tell Canwella that I'm going to the Monarch Club tomorrow. She doesn't seem convinced that it will knock anything loose, but I'm up for the challenge of seeing if I can perform where Nico couldn't. Especially when he made it clear that he seems himself as oh so superior to me.

Also, this place looks like it could be the palate-cleanser I need. They serve a full course dinner in the evening, and the floor show is silk dancers. The kind that do gymnastics on long trains of silk that hang from the ceiling. And they're wearing clothes, which is a huge relief. I've seen more boobs, butts and big boys than I care for in the last few days.

Except for one. There was one I am definitely okay with seeing again. Also touching. And kind of melting on.

I smile, remembering Liam holding that dumb twig like it meant something special to him. Maybe I should go meet his mom.

I get off the phone with Canwella and put my laptop away, rolling into the warmth of Shit. He yawns, showing me rows of razor sharp teeth that snap shut into a shit-eating grin as he reaches out a delicate paw and boops my nose.

I can't believe I passed on round two with Liam in order to handle a Canwella breakdown and settle for a cuddle with a Dalmanther.

But Shit is cute, and I've got all the time in the world to make it up to Liam. I start planning exactly how I will do that, and fall asleep with a smile on my face.

25

———

I have never been an early riser, but noon is pretty lazy, even for me.

"Shit," I say when I roll over and see the alarm clock. A small yap meets my exclamation and I look at the floor to see that my dog has done his signature move—and namesake—all over my bedroom floor. I can hardly blame him though. I can't expect him to hold it all night and into the afternoon simply because Mommy got laid and needed a rest.

I'm smiling when I check my phone, and it gets wider when I see two texts from Liam. One saying how much he enjoyed seeing me last night, the other saying he can't wait to do it again. Another text follows fast on the heels of that one.

*I mean, **see** you again. I'm fine with just seeing you, too.*

The ellipsis pops back up and I let him stew a minute, enjoying his British manners.

*Of course, I want to **do it** again too...don't think I don't.*

And another text in response. *But that's not what it's about for me. I'm sorry I freaked you out with the meeting my mum thing. I just wanted you to know—I think you're special.*

And another quickly follows, *I'm a mess even over text. Ignore your awkward boyfriend.*

I let him off the hook, shooting back a quick, *Never gonna ignore you.*

I add, *Had a great time, too! Believe me when I say I will both see you and do you again very soon.*

I don't mention the whole mom thing. I'll deal with that later, but right now, I've got to focus. As much as I'd love to take part in the full course dinner at the Monarch Club, I can't say for absolutely certain that Romy isn't in danger, and waiting to investigate just because I want some prime rib doesn't seem like a good work ethic.

I go downstairs and study the wall that Shauna plastered with information about the Monarchs. Turns out they've got a decent happy hour with cocktail weenies and some butter-fly-shaped puff pastries that reviewers say are to die for. Shauna even worked up a little bio for each of the employees. "The ones circled in red would probably go for you," she tells me.

I turn with a jump and look into her eyes. Wait a second, usually I have to look down at Shauna's tiny face. "Didn't see you there...Holy shit, are you levitating?"

"Yeah," yawns. "It's a vampire thing."

"That's incredible," I kick my foot under her floating legs.

"No biggie," she says. "You know I can actually fly, right?"

"With wings, not just..." I move my hands. "Woo woo magic."

Shauna rolls her eyes, "Sometimes I forget how human

you are. I used to hate humans. But I like you. Or I did. Are you always this annoying?"

"I know you're trying to kick beauty so I won't punch your pixie ass across the living room," I tell her.

"Thanks. I am in a pretty bad mood. Can you give me a push, though, toward the couch?"

I do, and she floats away, collapsing onto a pile of blankets and pillows. "Do you want to go into your room?" I ask. "I guess I could carry you. You weigh hardly anything, even without the creepy vamp floating."

"Nah," she says with a grunt. "I don't have a TV in my room. And I want to watch my programs." Shit jumps up on the couch and snuggles in with her.

"Okay, then," I say as I go back to the research wall. There's a lot of info, including a bit about their shady dealings. Mostly extortion, protection racket, stolen goods, and all the money funneled through their club, so it can come out squeaky clean.

I grimace at that, remembering Harmargan's description of how the Monarchs do away with their enemies, wrapped in a cocoon of sugar water. This place might look clean and fancy, but that doesn't mean that the management is any less dirty than Harmargan when it comes to doing business.

I find a cute little black and white pantsuit—complete with requisite bow tie—in Darron's closet. Luckily he's off lifeguarding at the retirement home and I don't have to do any explaining. I make a hard vow not to spill anything on this and have it back in his closet—fully ironed—before he's back home.

Shauna, still a pile of despondency on the couch, gives me a onceover as I leave the house and calls after me, "You look like you're going to a wedding...or a funeral," as I shut the door.

The Monarch Club is downtown, and I'm held up in traffic for a moment. Vanna always tries to observe road rules and manners, so instead of honking, she heats up my seat to an uncomfortable degree.

"What?" I ask her. "What did I forget?"

Vanna is better than the calendar on my phone about reminding me of where I need to be, with who, and what. Although her methods of getting my attention can be a little uncomfortable. But I feel like I've got all my bases covered. I'd even stopped at the office and checked in on Vee before heading for the club. Nico must have had a hard night out as well. His offices were closed and locked.

Oh...Nico. I'd promised him I'd keep him in the loop. Great. This is going to be a fun phone call.

"Thanks, girl," I say to Vanna, then tell my phone to dial Nico. The heat under my butt immediately goes down a few degrees.

He picks up on the first ring. "Let's keep it simple. Just tell me where you are and I'll come save you."

"Nice try," I snap. "I don't need saving. I'm actually covering your ass, it so happens."

"My ass is currently not covered at all," Nico says calmly, and I get the image of him in bed. Naked.

"Anyway," I say loudly as I switch lanes. "I'm headed to the Monarch Club."

"You've got a bow tie?"

"Yes," I say stiffly. "And I'm not sending you a pic."

"Fair enough," he says, and a yawn follows. I do think he *is* in bed. "Nico Tralano, are you taking a nap?" I ask.

"I am," he says, and I hear the sheets rustle. My mind wanders to what they're made of. Is Nico an Egyptian cotton kind of guy, or does he go silk?

"Rough night?" I ask with a smirk.

"Yes, but not in the way you're insinuating," he says. "I was out looking for VSK."

Even though I know now Liam isn't VSK, a little shudder passes through my body. At least when I thought it *might* be him, I had a good idea of who I should be scared of. Now...it could be anybody leaving their trophies on my front porch.

"He's been quiet for three days," Nico says. "That worries me."

Three days? Is that all it's been since my last gift? It feels like forever. I guess time works differently when you're measuring it in serial killer run-ins rather than hours and minutes.

"Why would that worry you?" I counter, as traffic picks back up. "Shouldn't you be glad he's not on the prowl?"

"Oh, he is," Nico assures me. "He's just not shooting up signals. Something has him busy, and that makes me uncomfortable."

It does me, too, and I shift in my seat as I pull into the parking lot at the Monarch Club. "Oh hey," I say offhand. "Canwella thinks Romy was kidnapped."

"Yeah, she wasn't," Nico says, and I feel a little rush that my instincts were on point.

"How do you know?" I ask, probing.

"That note was about money, nothing else. It wasn't a threat. Romy is a young ogre; she's off doing her own thing and Canwella can't see that because she's a mom."

"How do you know about the note?" I ask.

"Canwella called me after you brushed her off last night," Nico says, stifling another yawn and the little rush I'd felt disappears.

"Nice," I mutter. "Good to be trusted."

"For what it's worth, I backed you up," Nico says. "And she did call me second. I am *under you* on this one, after all."

"Thanks for that," I say, letting the innuendo slide. I've got to make sure I keep Nico neatly sidelined. Liam is the man for me, and I'm not going to let some smug, one-eyed private dick flirt his way into changing my mind.

Another call comes in and I see it's from McGinnis.

"Gotta go," I tell Nico. "I'll let you know what I find out at the Monarchs."

"Careful, Paige," he growls. "They're not what you think."

"Yeah, yeah, I know," I say. "Catheters and cocoons, check. I've done my research this time. Lesson learned."

"I could teach you a thing or two..."

I hang up with Nico still talking, which is oddly satisfying, and switch over to McGinnis.

"Hey kiddo," he says. "Just letting you know your boyfriend checked out, after all."

It takes me a second to process what he's saying. "What? What do you mean? You already told me his record was clean."

"Don't get mad," McGinnis says, and immediately my temperature spikes up. Starting a sentence with *don't get mad* is a surefire way to make me livid.

"What did you do?" I seethe.

McGinnis sighs. "It didn't sit right with me, not checking him out. I know you said you'd made the decision and you trusted the guy, but I didn't."

"You broke into his place, didn't you?" I ask.

"Paige, something about him had me on edge. I couldn't just ignore that. I'm a cop, and you're my friend. I didn't want you walking into the lion's den, and me just waving and telling you to have a good time."

"I did have a good time," I tell him, teeth clenched. "And I didn't need you as backup!"

"I did what I thought was right," McGinnis says, his voice suddenly cold.

"Which was exactly what I told you not to do!" I shoot back.

Oh God, was he in Liam's apartment at the same time I was reassuring him that he could trust me? What if I had taken a shot at a second round of sex and gone home with Liam? McGinnis could've been skulking in a closet somewhere. I feel sick. I feel...violated.

"I hope it helps that your instincts were right on," McGinnis keeps going. "I didn't find anything concerning."

"It doesn't help!" I say. "I'd already made that decision, and I don't need your approval! You're not my dad!"

It slips out of my mouth before I can stop it. I'm so angry I can't see straight.

I told him to leave Liam alone, and instead he broke into his place. I'm the only person that makes decisions about my love life. Not McGinnis. It could've been catastrophic to the relationship if he'd been caught, and I would've had to explain that this older man only had my best interests at heart when he violated Liam's privacy.

"If you really want to help, you need to close down Super Au Naturel. There is a lot of shady shit going on in there, and I know for a fact that a few of your brothers in blue are getting bribed. Maybe focus on criminals and not so much on me and my love life."

"That's not fair," McGinnis says, his voice deadly calm. I must have really wounded him. "I know you're angry at me..."

"I have to go now," I tell him, hanging up. I feel a little bad; McGinnis has always had my back, but he crossed a line.

I'll have to tell Liam. He told me the truth and he deserves the same.

"Save me from men," I say into Vanna's steering wheel.

Then I check my reflection in the rearview mirror, and straighten my bow tie.

26

The Monarch Club lives up to its reputation.

Everything is spotless and glamorous. White tablecloths cover everything and I'm pretty sure I'm dealing with real silver and bone china as the maître d' leads me to a corner table for one. I spot a bar tucked along the corner and inform him that he can find me there for the next hour or so, to which he nods, and tells me that I'll want to make sure I'm at my seat when the floor show starts. Apparently it's a big deal and other diners dislike having the distraction of patrons moving around the room.

This is so different from Super Au Naturel—where everyone was moving up against, or into each other—that I'm feeling a little out of place as I slide onto a barstool. It's real leather, and swivels easily, not squeaking at all.

The bartender, a young Monarch—luckily one that Shauna had scoped out as someone who would be easily "seduced"—glides up to me, eyebrows raised. "And what can I get the lady?"

Again, Shauna's brief on the drink menu helps me out. My usual Jack and Coke might earn me a bounce out of here. Instead, I order the nectar, which is the most expensive drink...and the one that will get me in his good graces the fastest. I sip it gently—it's too sugary for me, but I make a mental note to bring Shauna here. Then I reassess that, remembering that Shauna is off sugar...and most of the things in here look breakable.

Even the bartender. He's small and slightly built, the tattoo of a butterfly inside his wrist fluttering with his movements as he pours. The nectar has warmed my throat, but also my brain. I feel a tickle of recognition at the sight of the tattoo, and remember the girl dancing at Au Naturel.

"I like your ink," I tell him, when he passes by. "It's nice and understated." I show him mine, of Ursa Minor, and he gently holds my wrist in his hand, inspecting it.

"Tasteful," he decides. "Not like some humans."

"You'll find I'm not like most humans," I say, tipping my cup at him. He refills it when I put it down, and I make a note to drink more slowly this time. Nectar apparently has a very high alcohol content along with the sugar.

"Who did yours?" I ask, keeping the conversation light, and about tattoos. I don't exactly know how I'm going to segue into, hey, I heard you all got robbed? And also—know anything about a wandering lady ogre?

"Specialty," the bartender says, flickering his fingers so that the bones on his wrist move under the tat, making it look like the butterfly is fluttering its wings. I can't say if there's some magic involved with the ink, or if I've had too much nectar already.

"Charming," I say, accidentally mimicking Liam's posh accent. I clear my throat and go back to the Jersey girl voice that is truly me. "I want one."

"Sorry," the bartender says, shaking his head. "This tattoo is reserved for Monarchs only."

I let out a laugh. "Tell that to any twenty-year-old looking to get an ankle tat," I tell him.

"This design is ancient," he schools me. "It's the Monarchs' family crest. Only family gets this design."

"Oooh, sure, like the Russian mobsters that get special tattoos that mean different things." I laugh again.

"Something like that," he tells me.

I stare appreciatively at his wrist, then I cock my head for a second, thinking hard. I know I've seen this very same butterfly tattoo on someone that wasn't a Monarch. But the nectar has me sliding off the leather seat, and I have to move quickly to make it look like it was on purpose.

"Ladies room?" I ask, and he points the way.

I try not to weave as I push open the door. The bathroom is just as tasteful as everything else in this place. Everything is airy wrought iron and bright porcelain. I take a tinkle and throw some cold water on my face, hoping to counteract the nectar. This isn't quite as bad as the time somebody spiked my drink with incubus sperm, but I'm certainly feeling the effects.

I give my hair a toss and leave the bathroom, only to hear raised voices coming from behind a door marked "Office." I stop and pretend to straighten my bow tie in one of the many mirrors that line the hall.

"I'm telling you, Jimmy. He's gone. Searched his room. Searched the club. Julio is gone. Vamoozled, like the humans would say."

I bite my lip, trying not to laugh. Supes always mess up human sayings. Sounds like this Monarch is making a mix up of *vamoosed* with *bamboozled*. And while it's cute, it's also...very interesting.

Jimmy is the head of the Monarch crime family. Julio is his son. And he's missing. Just like Romy.

I lean in further but tip into the door, accidentally bursting into a tasteful office. Everything is wood and shiny. Two older gentlemen look up at me. Both are slight, but the one behind the desk holds himself like he's ten feet tall.

"Oh!" I put my hand up to my mouth. "I'm so sorry. I thought this was the ladies room!"

"Yeah, that's why the door has office on it," the one who isn't Jimmy Monarch says.

"Does it?" I giggle. "Sorry!" I back out smiling. Shutting the door, I wait a second to make sure they're not following me. I hear Jimmy Monarch say, "dumb broad," and then can't understand what else they're saying. It's sexist as shit, but the dumb girl act can get a girl out of trouble in a pinch.

I step down the hallway, and a very elegant older woman in a sparkling dress walks up to me. I smile, knowing she is about to compliment my hair, or my outfit, or my bow tie.

"Honey, you have toilet paper on your shoe," she tells me conspiratorially.

"Oh, no." I reach up my foot to grab it off, and almost fall over before I catch myself on the wall. But it's not toilet paper, it's a scale. The same kind I found at Charms.

I take my stool back, put the scale into my purse, and see that the bartender has freshened my glass. The service here is top-notch, but I'm not exactly thrilled about it. Maybe they have some kind of policy about getting the humans as smashed as possible. Or maybe this is the oldest trick in the book and he's just running up my tab.

Regardless, I've got to play nice if I want to learn more.

"Sorry to disappoint you," the bartender says, rejoining me. "About the tat," he clarifies, when I clearly don't follow.

"It's very attractive," I allow, but I've got to find a way to move this around to something that serves my needs more.

"Lots of girls would do anything for one," he goes on,

wiping a glass. "I've seen marriages based on less. So if you really want one…"

He tips me a wink.

It's not badly done, but I could also probably break him over my knee. Plus I think it's possible he wasn't born until I was in college. But I can play along.

"I don't know if I'm the marrying type," I tell him, but I purr a little, and he leans in. "Can't, you know, just make an exception?"

"Sorry," he says. "Rules are rules. Gotta either be a Monarch, or married to one, if you want a tattoo like this."

"I'm not married to a bear shifter, and I've got this," I say, raising my wrist. It's awkward and silly, but he follows me.

"You're not married at all," he says, glancing at my left hand. "Don't think I didn't notice."

Aw, poor kid. "You're adorable," I tell him, keeping it light. "But I really came here to see Julio."

He jumps back as if I'd electrocuted him. "You're Julio's girl? Sorry! I'm… so sorry. That's…I can't… "

He's wiping the glass so fast now it's going to have an indentation in the side.

"Hey," I say softly, reaching out to touch his hand. "It's okay. I won't tell."

But he pulls back from my touch. All flirtation gone as he wheels around to make sure no one is paying any attention to us.

"You're hot and all," he goes on, "but nothing's worse than getting on Julio's bad side. Don't want the boss's son pissed at me."

"No, can't have that," I agree, sipping my drink, confident now that I'm getting somewhere. A lot further than Nico Tralano had.

The bartender shakes his head and starts polishing the

bar near me, still interested enough for conversation but cautious enough to try to look busy at the same time. He drops his voice to a low whisper.

"The guys said Julio's mooning hard on somebody, really lost his head for a girl. Rumor has it he's in love." It's clear that he's now trying to butter me up. If I'm Julio's girl then that makes me powerful just by proximity, apparently. "Maybe you'll get that Monarch tattoo after all."

"Maybe, if I play my cards right," I agree.

"Well, don't forget the little guy once you're at the top of the ladder," he says. He glances at his watch and reaches for a tiny, silver bell resting on the bar. He rings it, the clear tones rolling over the whole club. Conversations settle as the lights dim.

"Floor show's getting ready to start," he says. "You'd better go back to your table."

"Thanks," I tell him, reaching for my purse, but he shakes his head.

"On the house. They'd cocoon me if they knew I charged Julio's girl for her nectar."

"I'd like to think it takes more than that," I say, with a light laugh. But he only looks at me as if I'm naive. I cut my losses, and wind my way back to my table, concentrating hard when I have to traverse the little steps down to my tier. I'm thrilled my nectar was free when I check the menu waiting for me at my seat. I can't afford this place.

When my waiter appears I ask if there's a bread basket "on the house." He gives me a weird look and then comes back with two large plates full of apps. "On the house, for you," he says, with a nervous smile. I guess the bartender told the waiter that I'm Julio's girl and now I'm getting free food. I'm tempted to put in an order for an entree too, but decide not to push it. Besides, the weenies and puff pastry that were in Shauna's report are just as good as the reviews stated. I've got a warm plate in front of me and a fresh nectar beside it before the silks fall from the ceiling, and the dancers begin their complicated moves.

They're all sinuous and muscular, lithe arms and legs twisting with the silks as they spin. It's mesmerizing, and I watch as a girl entwines her legs in her silks, swinging toward me, her costume gaping a little at the front.

She's built like a boy, so there's isn't much to slip out, but what does have is the same tattoo as the bartender—and the girl dancing at Harmargan's. Hers had been on her shoulder blade, but this silk dancer had opted to put hers on her breast.

Just like Romy's tramp stamp.

I stop, clenching my fork before the thought can slip away. I turn it over, thinking hard. That's why the bartender's tattoo had looked so familiar. It wasn't just because I'd seen it on the girl at Harmargan's. There'd been a flash of the same tatt that day in Seraphina's room—when Romy had been making use of her tub. Romy's breasts had floated to the top and I'd spotted her tattoo—one she shouldn't have unless she's part of a Monarch family.

The floor show is beautiful, but it doesn't have my attention.

Romy is missing. Julio is missing.

And I'm pretty sure they're secretly married.

27

As I drive home, I'm still debating what my next move should be. There's no way I'm sharing my suspicions with Canwella until I know for sure about Romy and Julio. From what Canwella's said in the past, I honestly think she'd be more worried about Romy marrying into the Monarch clan than she would be about her being kidnapped.

My plan is to check on Shauna and then head over to Charms and see if any of the girls know anything. Maybe Romy's confided in some of them. I'll need to get Canwella out of the way first—maybe I'll send her to some of Romy's favorite places.

As Vanna pulls into the driveway, I'm forced to quickly revise my plans. Officer Esposito is standing beside her car, all dressed up and looking annoyed that I'm not around.

Crap. I forgot all about her message about going clubbing tonight. I meant to cancel...but it's obviously too late for that now.

"What the hell, girl?" She demands as I slide out of Vanna. "You trying to stand me up?"

"I'm sorry!" I hold my hands out in a placating gesture. "I was working. Let me just reapply my makeup…"

"You're lucky I'm not wearing my ass-kicking shoes," Esposito grumbles as she follows me up the porch stairs.

No, her sky-high heels are definitely not for ass-kicking. But they are pointy enough to put another hole in it. Under the lights, I barely recognize the officer who pulled me over the other day.

Clearly, she likes to keep things buttoned up when working, but lets it all hang out during her off hours. And I mean it all hangs out.

She wears a dress tight enough to be painted on, while her dark hair hangs down her back in loose curls.

"You got ten minutes," she tells me.

"Absolutely, Officer," I reply.

"No, no, no, no." She clucks her tongue at me as her high heels click on the hardwood floors. "None of that officer stuff tonight. I am Eva, your dear twin sister. We finish each other's sentences. We—" She stops short as she catches sight of what I'm wearing.

"A bow tie?" she asks. "Are you serious with that?"

I'd honestly sort of forgotten I was wearing it. "I'll take this part off," I tell her, figuring the rest is okay for a night out.

But Eva is already shaking her head. "No way, girl. That is not gonna fly," she tells me in a way that leaves no room for disagreement. Swinging her tiny purse off her shoulder, she reaches into it and pulls out a piece of cloth. "Luckily, I brought you a dress to match mine!"

"Wow, that's so nice of you!" I say, certain I won't be wearing it. There's no way that tiny thing will fit me.

But it turns out I'm wrong. Eva calls it a one size fits all bandage dress and it does sorta fit. Or at least it goes over my head. Darron actually has to come down and help when I get trapped in the dress with my arms pinned over my head. Somehow, though, between him and Eva, they manage to pull it down over my body. I can already tell I'll be tugging at it all night trying to decide whether I want my ass sticking out of the bottom or my boobs popping out of the top of it.

"Well, it certainly leaves nothing to the imagination," Darron quips while I give him the evil eye.

"You're gonna have to cut me out of it when I get home tonight," I tell him.

"Um no way, girlfriend," Eva interjects. "We are going home with the cheetah twins tonight and he'll use his teeth to take it off you." She flashes her own pearly whites to demonstrate.

That's probably the moment when I should've informed Eva that I had no intention of letting a cheetah take me home. But I'm distracted when Eva adds, "Just don't fall for either of them. You can never trust a cheetah."

She says cheetah so it sounds a bit like cheater. I can't help but laugh. Eva laughs too in this sorta loud honking way that is oddly charming.

"Sorry," she says. "I can't resist a good pun."

"Never apologize for punning," I tell her.

"Ha," she laughs. "Not many people would agree with you on that. But whatever," she shrugs. "Haters gonna hate and former English majors gonna pun."

"You were an English major!?" I exclaim.

"So dumb, right?" Eva laughs that goofy laugh of hers again. "My parents told me I'd never find a job and they were right. But my dad was a cop and once I admitted my liberal arts mistake he was able to get me on the force."

"Same," I say, "Except my dad took me on in his cleaning business."

Somehow, without my quite meaning to, Eva and I bond the entire way to the bar. As we pull up in front, I no longer just feel bad about lying to get out of a ticket. Now I feel like I'm lying to a friend.

Shit.

I know that confessing to Eva now will ruin her entire night, so I decide to just go with it. The cheetahs will probably not even be interested in us anyway. There's no way they'll believe we're twins. Despite both having similar hair and eye color, that's pretty much where our similarities end. Eva is a petite little package while I'm taller and curvier. Much curvier. A part of me also suspects I'm the uglier twin, but I decide not to go there.

The bar is packed and a line stretches along the front wall. We pass it right by, though, the bouncer letting us through after greeting Eva by name. Inside the place has a slight barn smell to it and I'm not sure if that's by design or just an unfortunate side effect of so many animal shifters squeezed into one room.

Either way, I find myself trying to subtly breathe through my mouth. Moments later I'm screaming through my mouth as someone's hand slides up the back of my dress and squeezes my bare ass.

Okay, there isn't a whole lot of dress back there for the hand to slide up, but still that doesn't make it open season on my ass.

I spin around on my heel, ready to tear this guy a new asshole, when Eva screams, "Petey!" and throws her arms around the neck of Mister ass-grabber. He gives me a shit-eating grin over her shoulder, while I just glare.

Pulling away from him, Eva introduces us. "Petey is part of my hunting club," she tells me.

I frown, realizing this means the dude who pawed me doesn't actually have paws. Just regular human hands. Somehow this makes it worse, like shouldn't there be a little human to human respect?

"And Paige," Eva continues, giving Petey a wink. "Is my twin sister."

"Wow," Petey says with a low whistle. "You're the type that could tempt a man to settle down with a regular human gal." He clearly means this as a compliment, though someone should probably clue him in that 'regular gal' are not words to make a girl swoon. He follows this up by holding his hand out to me.

I leave him hanging long enough for his smile to slip and then wrap my hand around his—and squeeze. Leaning in, I tell him in a low voice, "You ever touch me again and I will mash your balls into a liquid pulp."

His eyes widen and then he pulls away with a sudden excuse about seeing a prospect across the room.

Eva gives me a look and I wonder if she'll be pissed that I just told her friend off, but instead she says, "He'll be good now that you've set boundaries. He's that type. Takes what he thinks he can get away with."

Ew. I wonder if Eva can hear how rapey that sounds. "He's a predator," I say to her.

"We prefer hunter," she says with a shrug and self-aware smile. "In the end though, we're all predator or prey." With her hand she makes a sweeping gesture around the room. "What do you think this is all about, anyway?"

It's a depressing thought and I can't help but recall that picture of Liam's father posing with his treasures. From what Liam told me, he thought of himself as a hunter too. The kind who turned his own son and wife into prey.

Before I can tell Eva that I want to live in a world a little more complicated than just hunter and prey, she nudges me with her elbow.

"Twin sighting at two o'clock," Eva squeals, grasping my arm. I look to where her gaze is directed and find myself staring back at...

Nico.

28

"Aren't they dreamy?" Eva breathes beside me.

Somehow I manage to tear my attention away from Nico's one eye and the way it seems to take in all of me—and I mean ALL OF ME—with a single sweeping glance. His eyebrows rise along with the corners of his mouth.

Beside him are two very handsome men who are indeed identically gorgeous. Unfortunately, they're wearing polo shirts with popped collars and identical self-satisfied smiles. Everything about them exudes superiority.

"Tech or finance?" I ask Eva.

"Huh?"

"Which one do they work in?"

"Oooh." She hesitates and then admits. "Finance. Some big Wall Street firm."

"They're assholes," I tell her. "They probably don't even care about the twin thing, they just want to make women jump through hoops."

Eva levels me with a look. "You're kinda killing my buzz here."

"Sorry, it's just..." This is my moment to come clean, but instead I gesture toward Nico. "I know that guy they're with. We sorta—"

Eva doesn't wait to hear the rest. "You know Nico Tralano?"

"Um...yes?"

"O.M.G." She breathes out each letter like the act of saying the full words is just too much for her. Seeming to gain control of herself she puts a hand to her chest and asks, "And have you landed the Moby Dick?"

"I...what?" Okay, I'm pretty sure I know what she's talking about—English majors of a feather and all that. But still, I want her to spell it out.

"He's the white whale," she tells me, confirming what I suspected. "The private dick we'd all like to land. But nobody rides that D unless they are down and out. It's like he's some sexual Robin Hood, only giving it to the ladies who are super hard up and broken."

"You're mixing your literary allusions," I tell her, while at the same time my head spins with this new information. I've assumed that Nico was easy, banging every client that came through his door. But does it see it as more of a public service? A way to help his clients onto their feet by putting them on their backs first?

It's kinda sweet in a way. But also totally arrogant that he thinks all those women need his magical healing wang.

"Fuck literary allusions," Eva says, which are pretty strong words for a former English major. "I want him so bad he scrambles my brains." She glances over her shoulder and then grabs my arms and gives me a shake. "He's looking at you, Paige. Like staring. Like he wants to take a bite out of you." Her eyes bore into mine with a scary sort of energy. "If it can't be me, then it's gotta be you. You'll just have to give me all the details—"

"Not gonna happen," I say and I don't know if I'm talking about banging Nico or sharing the details of said banging with Eva. But it doesn't matter, because she's not listening to me anyway.

"I'll be the Ishmael to your Ahab—"

"You do know how that book ended?"

"And you're gonna take down Moby Dick!"

I shake my head, realizing I won't be able to reach Eva with logic or literature. "What about the cheetah twins?" I ask, gesturing their way.

She flaps a hand at me. "Oh I've already had them, I just thought you needed it. You just had this really sad and desperate energy coming off of you. But now!" She grins at me. "You're gonna bag and tag Nico Tralano. And it's gonna be legendary."

Before I can object or try to inject some small bit of sanity, Eva is dragging me across the bar.

"Work that *poor pathetic me* thing you have going on," she coaches as we squeeze between gyrating patrons. "I think he's super into the pity fuck."

I don't have time to object to the *poor pathetic me* jab, and it's just as well because suddenly Nico is right in front of me, sitting on a barstool with both of his legs open wide in full manspreading mode.

"Hey," I say, "Funny meeting you here."

"Perfect," Eva hisses into my ear from behind me. "Totally lame line. Keep using that loser energy."

Gritting my teeth, I pull Eva up beside me. "This is my friend, Eva."

"We've met." Nico gives her a short glance. "She told me her husband had run out on her, but it turns out she's never been married and also forgot to put clothes on underneath her trench coat, which somehow slipped off during our initial meeting."

Totally unashamed, Eva just grins. "Can't blame a girl for trying." Planting a hand in my lower back, Eva shoves me toward Nico. I stumble forward and just barely catch myself by grabbing onto his thighs. Bent over like this, I can feel my dress exposing half my ass. Standing, I give it a sharp jerk...and my boobs spill over the top of my dress.

Nico's eye goes wide and then darkens in a dangerous way.

It's so insanely hot. I can feel the want radiating off him. And it's impossible to keep my own body from responding. My mouth goes dry and my nipples tighten to hard little peaks. Of course, Nico's eagle eye immediately sees that too. He growls low in his throat, more vibration than sound.

Somewhere nearby Eva continues to chatter. "Paige has had such bad luck with men. She's just been burned and burned again. I feel like she just needs some tender loving, ya know?"

Somehow Nico tears his eye from my breasts and finds my face again. "Is that right, Paige?"

Eva nudges me with all the subtlety of a matchmaking mother from a regency romance novel. "I'm gonna give you guys some space," she says and then grabbing the pair of cheetahs she pulls them both onto the dance floor.

I pull my dress up so that I'm once again sorta covered. Nico watches my hands, not even bothering to disguise his hunger. Now, though, I can't help but wonder...is Eva right and he gets turned on by pity fucks? Is that his attraction to me—that I'm such a hot mess?

It should be a turn off. It *is* a turn off. Except...Nico's gaze is so hot that my libido doesn't quite understand why Nico's reasons for wanting me matter. It just chants: *wantwant-wantwantwantwant.*

I remind myself that I had sex yesterday. Quite lovely sex. Oops, there I go sounding like Liam again.

Liam! His name is like a bucket of cold water, instantly cooling me.

Trying to shut it down, I say to Nico, "She dragged me over here."

He nods. "I figured."

"You're the Moby Dick," I add.

This earns a wry grimace. "So I've heard."

"She wants to be the Ishmael to my Ahab."

"That..." Nico frowns. "Doesn't the whale win in the end?"

I nod. "Moby Dick sinks Ahab's ship."

A wicked grin lights up Nico's face. "And Eva wants me to sink your ship."

I don't know how, but he makes the phrase sound dirty. A whole host of pornographic images flash through my mind as he lets those three words roll off his tongue.

"Uh-huh," I say stupidly. LIAM, I remind myself again and then quickly, I add, "But that's not gonna happen."

"No, of course not," Nico easily agrees. It's almost disappointing how quickly he agrees. My heart sinks despite myself. But then he adds, "But she doesn't need to know that."

"What?"

Again, that wolfish grin covers his face, changing it entirely, making him almost irresistible. "It's fiction, Paige," he says, putting his hands on my hips and bringing me closer so that I'm between his spread legs. "We let her believe the story she wants to hear."

I swallow. Hard. "She told me she wants all the details."

"Okay," Nico nods, like this makes total sense. "Then let's give you something to talk about."

And then Nico kisses me.

Whether he's playing with me or pitying me ceases to matter the moment his lips touch mine.

No, actually, even before that. First I feel the scruff of his chin against my own. It must be the wolf in him that gives him a permanent five-o'clock shadow. There's a moment—a half second—to push him away.

But I don't. The thought doesn't even cross my mind.

Instead, I close my eyes and breathe him in, too caught up in Nico's spell to do anything else. It reminds me that even normal humans are animals too. We have needs. Urges. And itches that must be scratched.

Nico is not a gentle kisser. His hands slide up into my hair, ruining my perfect high ponytail—not that I care in this moment. He tilts my head sideways and back, seeking the perfect angle for our mouths to connect. But the best parts are the little growls of frustration each time we have to —ever so momentarily—pause for breath.

Somehow my hands have gotten away from me and burrowed their way beneath Nico's shirt. I slide my hands over the ridged muscles covering his stomach on a southward journey to—

Nico jerks away. Breathing hard, his eyes have the distant look of someone who's just woken up from a dream. Or a nightmare.

29

---

*A*s for me, I am tormented with an everlasting itch for things remote. I love to sail forbidden seas, and land on barbarous coasts.

That's a quote from Moby Dick. But it could also be taken directly from my life.

My hands are stalled on Nico's abs and are still itching to move lower. Forbidden seas, indeed.

Nico is still looking at me as if he's hungry, but there's something else in his head that's keeping him from continuing our kiss.

"What's up with that British guy?" he asks. And there it is. The other thing in his head was Liam. The guy who should be taking up space in my brain. And heart. And...hands.

Quickly, I whip my hands out from under Nico's shirt and clench them at my sides.

"Who?" I say, stalling.

"Liam, right? The one you made a big show of kissing the other night. Just like you're now making a big show of kissing me."

I go cold. And then scalding hot. With embarrassment. Rage. And I don't know what else.

"Yeah," I say, feeling my voice with every bit of ice that I can gather. "The only difference is that with Liam it wasn't a show, it was real."

"Is that so?" Nico asks, a hard edge to his voice.

I put my chin up, refusing to be cowed even if a part of me is near tears. We were kissing and it was so good—until Nico pulled the plug. I feel like a fool for being sucked in. He played me.

And I feel even worse for betraying Liam. How could I ever look his mother in the eyes now? What is wrong with me? I could have a real future with Liam, and I'm ruining it. The only thing I see myself having with Nico is a sandwich. And even then there's a good chance I'd throw it at his head.

"Liam is the perfect man," I tell Nico, spitting the words in his face, wanting to convince myself as much as him. "He's sweet and sensitive, but also super hot between the sheets." This last part is true, though not in the sense I want Nico to believe. The one time Liam and I shared an actual bed, he made me so toasty warm I had to kick off the covers. But our sex was hot. Not scalding hot, but more like a hot bath. Comfortable rather than dangerous.

"I see," Nico says with a nod, coming to his feet so he looms over me. His hand comes to my cheek and gently smooths over the skin, leaving a trail of tingling skin in its wake. "Just so you know, this imperfect man standing in front of you just left beard burn all over your face."

With that, he turns on his heel, leaving me alone at the bar.

I turn away, not wanting to watch him go. Not wanting to call him back. Not wanting to be the Ahab to his big Moby Dick.

"Struck out?" Eva asks, suddenly at my side.

"Kind of…" I turn to her. I'm sick of this, playing someone I'm not.

"It's okay, let's focus on the cheetah boys. I hear they're fast, but thorough."

"Look, Eva…" I pull her over to the bar and order two shots. I fumble in my purse for some cash but come up with exactly seventy-eight cents. Shit.

Fuck it. I down the shot, and slap my purse on the bar. "Drink that." I tell her. I lean over the bar and shout at the bartender to put our drinks on Nico Tralano's tab, then order two more shots.

"Liquid courage?" Eva asks.

"I have to tell you something," I say, downing another shot of Jäger. I swallow the sickly taste down.

"I have a boyfriend."

"Okay…are you polyamorous? Or are you just a cheater?"

"Neither!" I take a deep breath. "He's human. I'm not a shifter groupie."

Eva laughs, then orders more shots—red headed sluts. "I wondered when you would admit that."

"I…you knew…?"

"That you were bluffing? Of course I did. I'm a cop. Want to be a detective some day."

"But you played along," I say, incredulous.

"Sure. I was very curious how far you'd go. I mean, would you have had a foursome with me and the cheetah brothers? Just to get out of a ticket?"

"I don't think you fully appreciate how broke I actually am," I tell her.

She laughs. "Look, I'm into hunting for shifter strange, but if you're not just say so."

"I'm so not," I admit.

I down one last shot, is this four or five? Plus what I drank at the Monarch Club. I'm getting a bit slurry. "You know what I really want to hunt down? Some pissa! Pisha. Pizza!"

"Yeah, let's get some food. I can always score another night."

"Sorry to ruin your hunt," I tell her. "I really do want to be friends with you. Especially now you know the truth."

"We can still be friends," Eva assures me. "You seem like an interesting person to know."

"I *am* intereshing. Esting. Interesting," I tell her. "I am a fucking barrel of laughs."

"All right, girl, let's get some food in you," Eva takes my arms and we go up the street to a little pizza place.

The pizza soaks up some of the booze and I start to think about my missing ogre and butterfly shifter. "Hey, let me use that detective brain of yours," I say to Eva.

"For what?" she asks, dabbing her lips with a napkin.

"Say you were a sheltered teenage girl, not allowed to have boyfriends or really go out…"

"That pretty much sounds like my adolescence," she tells me with a grin.

"But you didn't *not* go out right? You found a way?"

"Oh, I had my ways. Drove my parents crazy," she says, licking the grease off her fingers.

"Okay, so you're not allowed to date, but you have a secret boyfriend and you run off together…"

"That's some Shakespeare shit, right there," Eva says.

"Right, where would you go?"

"Where would two horny, repressed teenagers go?"

"Yeah, do you think they'd skip off, jump on a flight to Mexico or something?"

"No way," she shakes her head. "Not a couple of kids.

First off, it would be traceable. Second of all, they'd need a lot of money."

"They'd have money," I say with a sigh. "A ton of cash."

"Then my guess would be they'd find some low budget motel, some place that doesn't keep records, and check in until the heat dies down."

"Just check into a crappy motel?" I ask.

"Your not-so-hypothetical couple are probably screwing like rabbit shifters right about now."

"Oh shit," I say, dropping my slice. The image of the matchbook Romy gave me when I bummed a cigarette flashes through my mind. I can see the curly letters clearly, but not what they spelled out. Closing my eyes I concentrate. I remember thinking the name was a little bananas—MONKEY BUSINESS! My eyes snap open. "I have to go."

"What? Why?"

"I gotta ruin those not so hypothetical kids' night," I tell her.

"Do you need back up?" she asks.

"Nah, I can handle it," I stand up, but feel a bit woozy. "I can handle it after I eat more pizza and drink about a gallon of water," I tell her.

She grabs her purse and pulls a bottle out, giving it a shake. "Want one of these?" she asks.

"You're a cop...why are you offering me illegal drugs?"

She laughs. "Not illegal. Not even drugs really." She opens the bottle and shakes a pill out onto the palm of her hand. "It's a magic pill that will sober you right up. I have a witch friend who whipped them up for me. They are one hundred percent safe and effective."

She places the pill on my outstretched hand. "Trust me," she says. "I'm an officer of the law."

I shrug and swallow it down. Immediately I feel sober. I shake my head. "That is amazing."

I stand, grabbing my purse. "I'm sorry I have to bail but I really do want to hang out again. It's been fun," I tell her, and I actually mean it.

"Good luck, chica!" she calls after me.

I have to go to the Monkey Business Motel. It's time to save Charms.

30

I have an Uber take me home so I can change my clothes. The whole ride home all I can think about is Liam. He wanted to take things to the next level and I...

I went and kissed Nico.

What the hell is wrong with me?

By the time I get home, I feel like a piece of crap.

I change into jeans, a dark hoodie, and running shoes—not knowing what I'm going to go up against. Back downstairs, I look for Shauna, wanting to make sure she's okay before I head out again. Darron is already sleeping.

I find her in the kitchen with...Hepa from Harmargan's.

Her neck is lovely, long, and free of the magical collar.

"You escaped!" I exclaim.

Hepa shakes her head. "Not exactly. Super Au Naturel was raided. All the supes were freed."

"What?" My eyes go wide. "By who?"

"The cops, if you can believe it."

I can't believe it...but then I remember McGinnis and me telling him to go after them. He wouldn't...would he?

"She went to school with Tina," Shauna pipes up. Her face is bright and she looks happier than she has in a long time. "She thinks my plan to save her is totally reasonable."

Hepa rolls her eyes. "I said it wasn't totally insane."

"And she gave me this thing to track Brent," Shauna adds excitedly, holding up her phone. "Anywhere that shit takes a dump, I'll be watching." Shauna frowns. "I mean, I'm not gonna watch him go. But I'll know where he goes and when he goes. I'll know when he needs more fiber. I'll know when he ate a bad burrito—"

My head is swimming and this time it isn't from drinking. It looks like I'm gonna know a lot more about Brent's bathroom habits in the future. "Hold up, can we go back to the raid. Do you know who was leading it?"

"I thought you knew," Hepa's eyebrows go up. "The head detective said to thank you. What was his name...McGinnis, I think."

My legs wobble and I sit down in a chair. Hard.

I can't believe McGinnis did this for me.

"I guess Harmargan will be in prison," I say, as my brain races through all the ramifications.

Hepa gives a light little laugh. "I"m pretty sure they don't bother locking up corpses."

"He's dead?" I ask.

"Cops say he pulled a weapon on them, but I was right there. His hands were up." Hepa shrugs. "He had too much dirt on them; no way could they let him go to court."

I don't like this part of it. I mean, Harmargan definitely deserved to die, but did cops follow the law at all? And was it McGinnis who put the bullet in him?

"Shauna says I can crash here for the night," Hepa says. "Is that cool with you?"

"Of course," I agree. What's one more freeloader? "As long as you need."

"Yeah, it'll just be one night," she assures me. "I don't like other people enough to share space with them on a daily basis. Besides, there's some things I have to do, now that I'm free."

I tell Shauna to give Hepa the tour and get her settled in the guest room. Then I wander outside, still shaken by this new information. Climbing into Vanna, I'm about to back out when instead I say, "Vanna call—"

I mean to say McGinnis. To find out what he did and why. But instead I hear myself say—

"Liam."

"Paige?" He answers, sounding surprised and delighted by my call. Like I just made his night.

"Hey," I say, my voice softening and the tension draining away. "I know it's late…"

"Not at all, I was just thinking of calling you and asking if you'd like to come over. Or I could come to you. I don't want to presume, but I know you have roommates and my place is more private. On the other hand, there's little Shit—"

"Liam," I interrupt, laughing a little. "I'd love to see you tonight but I'm working."

"Cleaning?" He asks.

"No, um…investigating something," I say, realizing that I've started to think of this as my work too. Quickly, I catch him up on Romy's disappearance and where I think she is.

"You are brilliant," he says when I'm done and the way he says it—I believe it.

Warmth fills me. Not the heat I felt with Nico, the kind that left me ice cold when it was pulled away. This is something more lasting. Or it could be. If I let it.

"Liam, I want to meet your—"

My car door abruptly swings open. Nico stands outside Vanna looking dark and dangerous.

"I shouldn't have kissed you," he says, his voice rough.

"Nico—" I say, trying to stop him.

But he clearly isn't stopping until he's said his part. "You shouldn't have kissed me back. Or stuck your tongue down my throat. Or your hands up my shirt—"

"Nico—" I gasp. "I'm talking with—"

Oblivious, he continues. "But what you did isn't my responsibility. I gotta answer for what I did. The truth is, you get under my skin and I like getting under yours. But right now we're working together I shouldn't have let it happen. So..." He pauses and takes a breath. "I'm sorry."

I say nothing. There are no words. I just stare at him.

And then through the car speaker comes Liam's voice. "This is obviously not a good time to talk. So I'll just—"

The call disconnects.

Nico's eyes are wide. "Shit."

I look at Nico. "You didn't know he was on the phone with me?"

"I'm a wolf, not a rat."

I nod. And then realize that I have screwed up everything. My eyes fill with tears before I can stop them.

"Paige..." Nico's voice is low and full of regret. "I'm sorry."

I shake my head and wipe my eyes before the tears can overflow. "It's fine. I gotta go. Romy—"

Immediately, Nico straightens. "What about Romy?"

Feeling strangely numb, I answer, "I know where she is. And with who. Ninety-eight percent sure."

With a leap, Nico launches over Vanna's hood and then is jumping into the passenger side. "Let's go, then."

I'm too broken to argue with him, so I simply say, "Vanna, you heard the man. Let's go."

31

Nico takes charge, slipping the clerk a twenty. I left the bartender at the shifter bar the last change in my purse so it's probably best that Nico is handling the bribes.

"We're looking for the ogress," Nico says.

Romy is hard to miss, and the clerk knows exactly who we're looking for.

At the door, I move my hand up to knock, but Nico stops me.

"Hold up," he says, "I got a feeling."

I am so not in the mood for Nico and his wolf senses tingling. "Whatever," I start to say, when a shout from the other side of the door catches my attention.

"Don't think you can cross me and get away with it," a man's voice says.

I frown. Maybe Julio and Romy are doing some role play?

"I'll make you regret you were ever born," Romy responds, and the tone of her voice tells me she's not playing.

Well, that romance certainly went downhill fast. Maybe that's how they all go sooner or later, I can't help reflecting. They cheat on you. Or you cheat on them.

Oh hell. For the first time I realize this is exactly what I did to Liam when I kissed Nico. I cheated on him. Something I swore never to do after Jax broke my heart.

I am slime. I am dirt. I am—

"I'm breaking the door down," Nico announces. Before I can object, he throws himself forward. The cheap door shatters easily and we burst through into a room full of an ogress, a young man, and three men with a reptilian quality.

"The snake brothers!" Nico huffs.

Everyone one of them is holding a gun. And all five guns swing our way the moment they see us.

32

I t takes me a second to wonder if Nico means that the brothers are snakes, like jerks, or actual snake shifters. My guess is both.

The three guys are tall and skinny with bald heads that are sorta...scaly. The middle one seems to be really concentrating on holding his gun right at our heads. His tongue is between his teeth—making the fork at its tip easy to notice.

"Paige?" Romy says.

"Who's diss?" One of the snake dudes, hisses, which pretty much seals the deal on the snake thing.

"I'm the bitch who shut down Super Au Naturel," I announce, standing tall and trying to look like a powerful badass. "Get your guns out of my face or I'll take care of you the same way I did Harmargan."

The three snakes exchange glances. Romy, meanwhile, nudges Julio and they aim their guns back at the snakes and away from me and Nico.

"Okay," the head snake says, his gun still trained on me. "How did you take him down?"

"I'd be interested in knowing that too," Nico murmurs in a low voice.

I ignore him and focus on the snakes. I know them. They're the Snake Brothers Cleaners that were taking a bunch of jobs from me! "You disgust me. You're supposed to be a cleaning crew and you leave your scales all over the place."

"Who the hell are you?" the head snake asks, clearly bewildered.

"We can't help it," the littlest snake guy says. "Scales fall out when we shift."

"Then bring a handheld vacuum," I answer. "You can get one that charges in the car—"

The middle snake, the one with his tongue between his teeth, gasps. "She's that cleaning lady! The one who took our job at Charms!"

"Yeah, I am that cleaning lady. But I didn't take your job. You lost it by being sloppy and lazy. The same way you were sloppy and lazy when you robbed Charms and the Monarch Club. Why not just shed your skin too and leave a sign that says 'We were here. We did it!'"

"How did you know it was them?" Romy interrupts.

"I'm guessing she found some scales," Nico says. "Funny she didn't mention it to me."

I roll my eyes. "Don't be a baby, Nico, just because you've done nothing for this case but break down a door." I focus on Romy and Julio. Julio Monarch is super cute, thin and wiry. Standing beside him, Romy dwarfs him, but I can tell by the way they stand that they like each other. More than like. The two of them are clearly in sync. A team.

My heart clenches as I think of Liam who will probably never speak to me again. I could've had that. Why am I such an idiot?

"Paige?" Romy says, reminding me that I still have three guns pointed at me.

"I came here to get back the money you stole," I tell her.

"We're not giving it back," Romy tells me. "Julio and I are going to be together and you can't stop us!"

"Romy, I don't give a fuck who you...well...fuck. But Charms is going to be closed down. Your family business. Your mom thinks you were kidnapped. She is beside herself worried about you."

"Yeah right," Romy mutters.

Julio takes Romy's hand. "We didn't want to hurt anyone. We just wanted to be together."

Romy nods. "I didn't know how much money mom had in the safe. I didn't know it was EVERYTHING. I don't want Charms to be shut down."

"Well, you can return the money!" I say. "At least some of it."

"We can't!" Romy wails. "We were going to hit Charms and the Monarch Club, but we couldn't do it on our own. I'm too conspicuous. So we hired help."

I look at the snake guys. "Them, I assume."

Romy nods. "Those snakes took our whole stash and then they had the balls to come here and try to shake us down for even more."

"Babe," Julio puts his arm around Romy and she visibly melts a little. "Don't get all upset about this..."

"She has the right to be upset," I say, trying to get Romy to focus on me and not Julio. "Were these assholes trying to blackmail you for extra cash?"

Romy nods and I can see her fury growing. "They were gonna tell our parents where we are if we didn't commit a bunch of break-ins for them. They wanted me to do some smash and grabs, while Julio—"

"Babe—" Julio again tries to get Romy to calm down, but this time she shakes him off.

"Julio! My mother would die of shame if she knew I let a bunch of snakes push me around."

"Mine too—" Julio starts.

But Romy isn't finished. "I'm sick of sneaking around. We're married. I don't want to be your dirty little secret anymore. If you want me, then be with me out loud and proud or else—" Her voice distorts like she's leading up to an ugly cry. But the smell starting to waft off her tells me it's more than that.

"Are you ashamed to be seen with her, Julio?" I ask, needing to push Romy off the ledge.

"HE IS!" she screeches. And that's all it takes. I can't even say where the stuff comes from. Her pores maybe? All I know is that I barely have time to duck, cover, and whisper to Nico, "GO!" before the thick viscous goo squirts out everywhere.

I'll say one thing for Nico. He's good at taking orders. In the moment that the snakes are distracted by Romy sliming them, he shifts into his wolf form and is on top of them. Three armed snakes are nowhere near a match for werewolf Nico. The guns land at my feet, one after another, and then the snakes are cowering in a corner.

"It stinks," the leader hisses sadly.

"Yeah," I agree with him. "It really does."

33

TWO WEEKS LATER

"Hello, my name is Shauna."

How did I let her rope me into this? I shift in my chair.

"Hi Shauna," the circle of people choruses.

"And I lost my wife, Tina, in the Great Ghosting. It hasn't been easy. I got into drugs, big time. I actually come to the Magical Drugs Anonymous meeting on Thursdays and the Sugarholics meeting here on Tuesdays, and all this talking about my feelings instead of getting high is really helping me deal with grief."

"That's great, Shauna," the meeting leader tells her. "And I see that you've brought another friend?"

"Yes, this is my housemate and best friend in the world, Paige. Darron came last week, but he had to work this week, so I convinced Paige to tag along. I think she has some unresolved issues."

I squirm. By convince she means badger me into

submission. I try to disappear into the plastic chair, but no dice. Everyone is looking at me.

"I'm not sure I feel comfortable..." I start.

"It's fine. You can share when you're ready," the meeting leader tells me.

"Yeah, I'll share enough for both of us," Shauna assures me. "I actually can't stay long after because I have a playdate with my little nephew, Kit Junior," she tells the group.

It took some convincing, but Izzy said that as long as Shauna is clean, she can have a few hours a week with KJ. And if it works out, she can be a part of his life.

I am proud of Shauna and all the hard work she's been doing. Once she got over the slump of kicking beauty and sugar, she bounced back to normal. Well, mostly normal. As normal as Shauna can possibly be.

"I still miss Tina every day," Shauna is saying. "But I'm learning to make room in my life for people that are still here." She grins at me and I smile back. "Oh, and I made some date bars, sugar-free of course, I put them next to the donuts, if anyone is interested."

I could tell her that no one is interested, but there's no point.

The truth is, the group does make me feel better. Knowing that I'm not the only one who lost loved ones, hearing other people's stories, it really does help.

"See you next week, everyone!" Shauna calls after the meeting.

I offer to drop her at Izzy's but she tells me she'll Uber. I sit in Vanna, thinking.

The last two weeks have been relatively quiet.

Canwella paid me all she owed me and extra for bringing Romy back to her. I paid some bills and took

Darron on a shoe shopping spree, so now I'm back to being broke. It's okay, I'm used to it.

Romy's big disgusting outburst convinced Julio that it was past time to take their relationship public. They told his father about the relationship first, and then Canwella. Neither was happy about it, but both realized they had to accept it or lose their children.

Now Romy and Julio live in an apartment together exactly halfway between Charms and the Monarch Club. Romy is being trained in the backdoor dealings of the Monarchs while Julio has taken over the books for Canwella. Apparently, he's a whiz at finding different offshore accounts for her money. He's why the Monarchs weren't hit as hard by the robbery.

The guys and girls upstairs all sigh over the whole thing and say it's the most romantic thing they've ever heard.

I guess it is. But any talk of romance just makes me feel old these days.

Liam won't return my calls. Or texts. I've apologized and told him it was a mistake. All the same things Jax once said to me. So I get it if Liam can never forgive me.

But it still feels unfinished. I need to see him in person one last time. I need to hear him say to my face that it's over.

I'm so desperate to see him, I almost enlisted McGinnis's help. I figured he'd already broken into Liam's place once...

Luckily, I stopped that train of thought before it went any further.

McGinnis and I aren't that tight anymore anyway. He did spearhead the Super Au Naturel bust. According to him he called in every favor that was owed to him after nearly twenty years on the force. I was glad he did it, but I didn't feel like we were on the same page anymore.

I'm pretty sure I was the one who had changed. For so

long I thought that I didn't like the world that supes had created. But now I was seeing the human hands in it too.

The whole world was dirty. And it was too big for me to clean all of it up.

Since then, having anything to do with McGinnis has made me feel gross. Still, I know better than to ignore his calls. A few days back he rang with his usual, "Hey Kiddo," greeting.

Gritting my teeth, I barely managed to stop myself from asking him not to call me that. Just because I didn't want to be his friend anymore, didn't mean that I wanted him as an enemy. We caught up for a little bit. He asked if I was still with the serial killer's son. I lied and said that I was in love with Liam and meeting his mother soon.

McGinnis said he was happy for me that I'd found a nice man. It was almost a nice moment, because he did sound genuinely happy for me. But he ruined the vibe by putting extra emphasis on the *man* part. Like, what if I'd found a nice supe? Is that totally outside of his scope of the world?

Now, I'm heading home from the grief meeting when McGinnis calls again. I'm tempted to send him to voicemail so he doesn't kill my post meeting calm, but he'll just call again.

"What's up?" I say.

"Paige," his voice is hoarse and shaking. It makes me sit up straight.

"What's wrong?"

"VSK," he gasps. "Grabbed me right off the street. I got away, though."

"Holy hell, are you okay?" No one in my orbit, not even a cop, is safe.

"I'll be alright, but Paige...he had someone else in his

van. A guy with a British accent. I could hear him screaming."

"No," I whisper.

Vanna's tires screech as she takes a huge U-turn right in the middle of traffic. Cars around us brake and swerve to avoid hitting us. Amazingly, we get through unscathed though horns blare behind us as we take off down the street.

"I got away when VSK took the Brit out," McGinnis continues. "I kicked at the door until it flew open and then I ran."

Tears are running down my face. "Please say it wasn't him." I'm not even talking to McGinnis anymore. This is a prayer to whatever God or gods might exist.

"I'm so sorry, Paige. I was in bad shape. He drugged me. I climbed into a dumpster and passed out. When I came to, I called for help. It wasn't until they checked me into the hospital that I realized..."

"What?" I demand as McGinnis hesitates. "What?"

"The neighborhood I came to in, it was right near where your Liam lives. You said he was British..."

At that moment Vanna screeches to a stop in front of Liam's apartment.

"I gotta go," I yell and then I fly out the door.

I can hear my heart pounding in my ears as I take the steps up to the outer door. I throw it open and then turn to the left where...The door to Liam's apartment is cracked open.

"No."

I push it, my heart in my throat. Please, let it be that Liam just forgot to lock it and it popped open somehow.

"Liam," I call, surprised at how ragged my voice sounds. No answer. I take a deep breath and call out again.

Then I see him, on the ground, white as a sheet. I rush to his side and kneel next to him, cradling his head in my lap.

"Liam, wake up," I slap his cheek slightly. "Please wake up."

His eyes flutter open, but his gaze is glassy. I dial 911 with shaking hands, but when they ask what's wrong, I don't know what to tell them. "My boyfriend needs help," I say. "Just send an ambulance!"

I throw my phone in frustration. Why did VSK bring Liam here instead of leaving him on my porch like his usual MO?

Suddenly it occurs to me that maybe this is a trap and VSK is still here. He let McGinnis get away, knowing he'd tell me about Liam...

I spring to my feet. Terrified I'll see VSK stalking across the room, straight toward me.

Instead, I see a syringe on the coffee table. There's a note under the syringe. I grab it and read, my horror growing with each word.

P*aige,*
Would you prefer a dead boyfriend, or an undead one?
The choice is yours.

There's no signature, but I know who it's from. VSK. He's been planning this. I thought he lost interest in me. But Nico was right, he was just biding his time. And raising the stakes. This time he took two people—Liam and McGinnis. How ironic that they were the two people I've been the most distanced from in the past two weeks. But maybe that's why they were chosen; maybe VSK thought they had hurt me in some way.

"It's vampire venom," Liam says. His voice is so soft I have to lean my ear next to his mouth. "He bled me and said that he would let you choose. Turn me or let me die."

I grab the syringe. "Then I'm deciding. I want you to live."

"No!" he coughs out. "I told you, I don't want to be a vampire. I don't want to drink blood and be a thing of hunger and darkness. Let me go."

"I can't," I say, the tears streaming down my face. "This is all my fault. I can't just let you die." I grab at Liam's hand, desperate to convince him. "Remember Shauna is half-vamp, and you like her. Right? I mean, you hardly know she's a vamp. Just a few cups of blood a day and otherwise she's a totally normal—"

"Please, Paige," he begs. "Don't turn me. I can't." He takes a shaky breath and his eyes flutter, like he's fighting to keep them open. "Me being a vamp would kill my mum. She's never forgiven them. I can't do this to her."

Screw your mum, what about me? That's what I want to say.

But I have no right to say it. Or even think it. Despite what I told the 911 operator, I'm not Liam's girlfriend.

"Paige," Liam says my name once more, his eyes locked on mine, are clearly begging me to let him go. And then his eyes flutter closed.

He's dying. Nearly dead. Who knows how long he's lain here? I curl into Liam, putting my head on his chest, listening to his heart beat ever slower while tears stream down my face.

I can't let him die. I just can't sit here. He thinks being a vamp is awful. He thinks his mom won't get over it. But Romy thought her mom would never accept Julio.

My brain whirs, hunting for more justifications.

Liam's chest goes still. No more breath in. Or out.

It's now or never.

I hold up the syringe, but my hand wavers. Can I do this against his will? Can I make this choice?

My hand arcs down and I stab the needle into his heart.

I push the plunger down. There's no going back now.

VSK has won again.

THE END

———

Continue the series with the next book **The Lying, The Witch, and the Werewolf - book #4!**

Sign up for our newsletter to receive FREE short stories! Visit www.marleylynn.com/newsletter

Like us on Facebook for books deals, surprise sales, and promotions!
www.facebook.com/MarleyLynnAuthor

SNEAK PEEK: THE LYING, THE WITCH & THE WEREWOLF (DOWN & DIRTY SUPERNATURAL CLEANING SERVICES BOOK #4)

1

I turned my boyfriend into a vampire, and now he won't answer my calls.

Well, I say boyfriend, but it's been three months since I've seen him, so I think it's safe to say I'm officially dumped, and being dumped does not make a girl feel awesome...especially when I deserved it.

When I found him on the floor of his apartment, near death, Liam flat out told me to let him go, that he'd rather be regular dead than a member of the living dead. But I went against his wishes. I took that needle full of vampire venom and plunged it into his heart.

Maybe it was selfish. Maybe it was me holding onto the last bit of normality I had. But it doesn't matter now whether he's normal, nice, British human Liam, or sullen, moody, vampire Liam.

Because neither one of them is in my life.

Well, not willingly. I've been keeping tabs on him, either as a result of guilt, love, or my complete inability to come to terms with our sudden severance.

I sigh and park my van in front of the client's house, a

nice modern two-story with a ton of windows. The woman who called to hire me had sounded young, and with a voice so low and husky I'd almost hung up on her at first, thinking it was another prankster trying to get me to have phone sex with them. Dad did warn me about going with the pin-up look for the logo for the Down & Dirty cleaning business, but it earns me more work than headaches, so I'll take it. After chatting with the potential client a bit more, I decided she was legit. So here I am, ready for my appointment.

Before going in, I give my ex-sister-in-law and current housemate, Shauna, a call. "Any difference?" I ask.

"Liam's the same as he was yesterday," she tells me. "He hasn't left his room. He barely interacts with the other vamps in the house."

"Thanks for keeping an eye on him," I say. As a fae-vamp hybrid, Shauna has access to Liam's new world in a way that I don't. It's a lot to ask of her—three months of surveillance on my ex. But that girl owes me. She lives with me rent-free.

Like I said, my ex-human, ex-boyfriend was the last bit of normality I had.

"No problem, but it's starting to get creepy."

"I'm just concerned for him," I say, sliding into the back of the van and gathering up my supplies.

"Maybe the first week made sense for you to be concerned, when he lost his job and moved into a vampire halfway house," Shauna tells me. "Now it's getting stalkery."

"Don't joke about that," I say. I have my own stalker to deal with. VSK—the Vampire Serial Killer—is the whole reason Liam ended up like this. "Is he getting enough blood?" I ask, trying to dispel thoughts of VSK from my mind.

"They limit his blood intake," Shauna reminds me.

"Newly-turned vamps can go crazy with blood lust if they get too much."

"I know, I know," I say, slamming the van's door a little too hard. Vanna gives me a honk and I apologize. "Look, I gotta go. I guess you can stop shadowing Liam. He doesn't want to see me. And he seems to be under control."

"Okay, I'm going to hit up a Great Ghosting grief counseling meeting later. Wanna come?"

"No, I'm good." I've been to a few meetings with her, and though they make Shauna feel way better, they didn't really do anything for me.

"You can't just keep everything inside, Paige," Shauna starts and I roll my eyes. She was a hot mess after her wife disappeared along with a bunch of other people, including my parents. One second they were there and the next— gone. No reason. No explanation. Just poof. That was nearly three years ago. Shauna got big into drugs. Then her brother died. She was a flaming dumpster fire.

Now that she's clean—off the fae drug of choice, beauty —she thinks she's my personal life coach.

"Oh, gotta go," I say quickly and hang up.

Closing my eyes, lean against the van and allow myself a minute to feel my feelings.

The truth is, these last three months have been a struggle. My heart is like a rock inside my chest and the weight of it spreads to my limbs during the long afternoon hours. By the end of the day, my body is so heavy I can barely get up all the stairs to my attic bedroom.

I've had broken hearts before, but this is different.

If Liam had never met me his life would still be normal. Human normal, I mean. VSK targeted Liam because of me. He also went after my cop friend. Luckily, McGinnis got away, but he messed himself up pretty bad kicking his way out of VSK's car and now clumps around in one of those boot casts. The last update I got from him, he said he might even need surgery.

I can't stand the idea of VSK hurting someone else I care about. He's been quiet since he went after Liam and McGinnis, but I know he's not done. He's just biding his time. All I can do is wait and hope that the next person he comes after...is me.

In the meantime, though, the bills still gotta be paid.

I lug my bucket and cleaning supplies to the front door and knock. A handsome twenty-something man opens it and grins. He's covered in blood.

"You're here! That's great, just...small hiccup," he tells me, moving aside so I can enter the hall. "My wife is still in labor. I should have called, but it slipped my mind."

"You have more important things to deal with," I tell him, eyeing the bloody footsteps on the wood floor. He could have thrown a freaking towel down at least.

"It's coming," someone shouts. "The baby is crowning!"

He rushes off and I follow behind to a large bathroom. A woman is in a tub filled with crimson water, and blood coats the walls. Between her legs is another woman, who also looks about twenty-five.

I have no idea how old any of them actually are. Vampires don't age. If the wife's super sexy voice over the phone hadn't clued me in that my new employers were vamps, the smell of the powerful sunblock vamps use has done the trick. I smelled it as soon as I walked in the door, a little tang under the heavy smell of copper.

In a flood of blood, the midwife pulls the baby out and it cries, its wailing somehow endearing. My ears suddenly turn hot and I feel my face redden. The man rushes to his wife and I stand awkwardly to the side. I could come back later, but honestly, I'd rather scrub off the blood while it's still wet—less work that way.

The midwife turns and smiles at me. "Oh, looks like somebody might have a touch of baby fever!"

"What?" I ask, backing away, warding her off with my mop.

"You're flushed," she says, reaching for my cheek. Her palm is cool against my skin and I relax a little. "It's the hormones," the midwife confides. "Your body is reacting to the baby."

She gives me a quick once over, her vamp eyes assessing my human frailties. "You're what? Mid-fifties?"

"Thirties, thank you very much," I snap back.

"Sorry," she shrugs. "Vamps aren't very good at judging human age. But don't worry." She pats my wrist. "You've got time."

"I don't—"

"This must be a lot," she motions toward my mop and then around the blood-spattered room. It looks like someone was murdered here. Vamps have more blood inside their bodies than is scientifically possible. There's a particularly nasty gif circulating among the Humans First group of a vamp being hit by a car. He just kind of explodes like a water balloon. But one filled with blood.

"It's actually not my first vampire birth," I tell her and am pleased to see that now it's her turn to be taken aback. "I'll start on the hallway," I announce. "Then I'll tackle in here."

Some people hate cleaning, but I like it. It's satisfying to make something dirty look brand new. It also lets me focus on a simple, obtainable goal, instead of thinking about all the crappy things in my life.

Like my ex-husband Jax who is playing house with his

new witch girlfriend. Or my ex-boyfriend Brent who is a murderer and Humans First senator. Or the fact that a vampire serial killer is obsessed with me...and forced me to turn my boyfriend into a vampire or let him die.

Hmmmm, maybe I shouldn't call Shauna's life a dumpster fire. People in flaming bins shouldn't throw garbage.

By the time I clean the hall and start on the bathroom the happy new parents are all showered off and cooing to their new baby in the nursery. The woman looks like she just ran a 5k and then did a shampoo commercial, all sheeny and glowing. The dad looks at his wife and kid like they're the pot of gold at the end of a rainbow.

He catches me staring. "Sorry about the mix up. I booked you as soon as she started labor; I thought it would be like the others...done in twenty minutes." He laughs. "But this little guy had other plans!" He makes googly eyes at the baby and I can feel a tug at my heartstrings.

"How many other children do you have?" I ask.

"This is ten," the woman tells me. I look around. There's no indication of other children in the house.

"Our other kids are grown," the man tells me. "We like to wait at least thirty years before trying again. It makes things easier on us."

I nod. The couple do not look a day over twenty-five, but that's the age most vamps look. "How long have you two been together?" I ask, more to be polite. I'm eyeing the bathroom down the hall. It doesn't take long for all that bloody water to dry on the tile.

"We just celebrated our half millennium," the woman says, not taking her eyes off the baby.

I nearly drop my mop. "You've been together for five hundred years?" I ask.

The man nods. "A lot of vampires marry for political

gain, but we fell in love. And once a vamp falls in love, well, we're a fiercely loyal bunch."

I think of Shauna; she was born a fae and turned vamp, but she still loves Tina with a passion that I can only hope to one day feel for someone. I had thought Liam might be that person. And now he's not a person anymore. Not a human, anyway. Now that he'll live forever like any other vamp, it's totally possible he'll *hate* me for a half millennium. It's not exactly the mark I hoped to leave on the world.

I trudge to the bathroom and try to lose myself in my job but I keep thinking about the vampire couple being together for five centuries. My marriage to Jax didn't even last five years. My dating Liam lasted about five minutes.

"We read about you on Friendbook," the husband tells me from the doorway. "We appreciate all you're doing for the supernatural community."

"I just clean up people's messes," I tell him.

"That's not true. You helped that vampire get away from the mob at the Humans First rally a few months ago. Plus you shut down that awful supe adoption agency that was stealing babies. And Super Au Naturel, what a shithole. We never went there, but you hear things. You got that place busted up."

I look up at him. "I'm just really good at being in the wrong place at the wrong time," I tell him.

"Well, a lot of supes are talking about you."

"Greeeeat," I say. Business has picked up lately and my clients are all exclusively supernatural beings. I really do not feel comfortable being supe famous...especially if some of my old social media posts ever are dug up.

I wasn't exactly kind about the influx of non-humans when it first began. I've changed in a lot of ways, but my Dad and I started this business as a way to help other humans clean up after a supe trashed their house—or their lives. I never meant to become a housekeeper to the paranormals. But I have to admit, most supes are friendlier than the average human. And they pay better, too.

"Can I ask you about being a vampire?" I blurt out. "I know someone who was recently turned...

The man shakes his head. "Oh, that's tough. Turned vamps have a really tough time. Is he limiting his blood intake?"

I nod. "I think so. He won't really talk to me."

"That's normal. Turned vamps..."—he shudders—"they have it bad. It used to be that the vamp who turned another would be responsible for them. Make sure they didn't go off the rails and drain an entire medieval city. Since we were all exposed, things have gotten dire. Newly-turned vamps are turning others. It's terrible." He sees the look on my face but quickly adds, "There are programs now, though."

"He's in a house," I tell him, my voice grows thick with emotion. The halfway house is the best place for him, but when I picture him there, I know with a certainty, deep in the pit of my stomach, that he hates it. Years ago vamps tortured him and his mother. To be surrounded by them, to be one of them—I cut off the thoughts, knowing I'll just spiral into a dark place.

Clearing my throat, I add, "It's for newly-turned vamps."

"That's good. They know what they're doing." He turns to go back to the nursery but I call out to him.

"What's it like being with the same person for five hundred years?" I ask.

Eager to answer, he turns back around. "When it's the right person, it's fantastic. Honestly, it feels like time has flown by. I look forward to the next five hundred years."

I smile, though I'm sure it looks strained. "That is...so...great..." I say between clenched teeth.

Fuck vampires and their pure eternal love.

I mop up the blood and try not to think about how nice that actually sounds.

———

Continue reading **The Lying, the Witch & The Werewolf, Book #4!**

SNEAK PEEK: FIRE & FLOOD (MYTHVERSE #1)

My parents and sister are at the airport, getting ready to board a plane headed toward Greece. Meanwhile, I'm waiting to be checked out of the hospital.

I'm supposed to be on that flight with them—a three-month work trip that my archeologist mom organized. But two weeks earlier I came down with a virus that turned into pneumonia. This, combined with my lifelong mortal enemy, asthma, made breathing suddenly a lot harder. And then nearly impossible.

That's where the hospital comes in.

The doctors saved my life. And then totally ruined it by telling my parents I should stay home tucked under a blanket on my grandmother's couch so I could be all rested up for my senior year of high school come fall.

I honestly didn't think they would really go without me. No offense to my grandma, but she's pretty old and kinda wobbly. No way would my parents leave their sickly daughter with her while they were on a totally different continent.

"Leave me behind? Screw that," I'd laughed right after the doctor who gave me the bad news left the room.

No one else laughed. Mom, Dad, and my older sister Mavis just stared back at me.

I swallowed, not liking those looks. "Right?"

"Well, sweetheart—" Mom paused as she took off her glasses and began to clean them on the hem of her shirt. It's one of her favorite avoidance tactics. When I was ten and asked her what sex was, she polished so long and hard that she snapped them in half.

Suddenly I was worried.

"Dad?" I turned to my no-bullshit go-to guy.

"Sweetheart, we rented out our house. Not to mention that for Mom, it's a work trip."

"And I'm getting college credits for an internship," Mavis added. That one really stung. Mavis and I have always been close. Sure there's the usual sisterly bickering, but beneath that we genuinely like each other. I was looking forward to spending the summer together exploring Greece with her and hearing about her first year of college out in California. All year she only came home for Christmas and I missed her like crazy. But now she's heading off again. Without me.

I argued—eloquently, I believe, or as eloquently as someone who has to suck on an inhaler when they get too worked up—for my right to go on this trip. Sure, it was about having fun, but it was also about education, and opportunity and... and the fact that I'd already rubbed it in all my ex-friends' faces that I was going.

In the end, we compromised. And by compromised I mean they just decided.

They would go to Greece as planned.

I would stay with Grandma and she would teach me

how to knit. Which was also, Mom pointed out, a learning opportunity. They presented me with a big cotton bag filled with a rainbow's worth of yarn and my very own pair of knitting needles.

It was one hell of a consolation prize. But I wasn't raised to be a sore loser, so I forced a smile and a thank you. Somehow I even managed to wish them well on their travels. Did an evil voice deep inside wish them months of chronic diarrhea? Maybe. But at least I didn't say it aloud.

Maybe I can knit them some diapers.

Now, I hold my bag of knitting supplies as a nurse wheels me out to the curb where my grandma waits behind the wheel of her '85 Lincoln. As I settle myself in the passenger seat my phone bings with a text.

MAVIS: We just boarded.

MAVIS: Didn't get seats together, but luckily I've already made friends.

A pic follows this second text. Mavis and some unbelievably good-looking guy grinning into the camera.

That is so typical Mavis. Even her bad luck turns out good. Stuck by herself and ends up next to one of the hottest guys in the universe.

The car jerks sideways and thumps up onto the curb and then down again. My phone flies out of my hand.

"Almost got that sonofabitch!" Grandma yells, giving her steering wheel a slap that I can't decide is meant to be congratulatory or an admonishment. I look back to see an alligator sunning himself beside the ditch at the side of the road. Gran hates them ever since they ate her Bichon Frise, Elsa, and attempts to mow them down with her car whenever possible. "Next time, next time," she mutters.

"Hey Grandma," I say, in my best poor pathetic left

behind tone of voice. "Maybe I can drive the rest of the way home? Get some practice in? It would really lift my spirits."

Grandma shoots me a look that is clearly meant to convey she may be seventy-three, but she ain't senile yet. "Sweetheart, you've failed that driving test what is it...eight times now? Didn't the last tester beg you to quit before you killed someone?"

"Grandma, I know how to drive," I protest. "I'm just a bad test taker."

I'm actually epically terrible. I tend to freeze up in high stress situations. And there is no situation more stressful than trying to go where you want without having to beg Mom or Dad for a lift.

"You're sick, Edie. What kind of grandma do you think I am? Why not rest a little bit on the way home? You look a little peaked." The light changes and Grandma floors it, slamming me back into my seat.

Another battle lost. It's true, though, I am tired. I close my eyes and try to pretend I'm on a plane. It's lifting up into the sky, to travel across an ocean, before finally settling down in the land where gods were born.

———

As we pull into the parking lot behind Grandma's condo the typical Florida afternoon downpour begins. Grandma slowly totters along while holding her little old lady umbrella that she always keeps in her handbag over my head so I don't get soaked and end up back in the hospital. It's nice and all, but I'm about three feet taller than Grandma so I end up just kind of walking hunched over to get under the umbrella, which doesn't make my chest feel too hot.

Finally we get into the creaky old elevator. It grumbles and lurches its way up to the sixth floor. By the time Grandma unlocks the door all I want to do is cry.

"What's that face for?" Dad asks.

I gasp. He's seated at Grandma's breakfast bar with a cup of coffee. Not on a plane to Greece—but here.

"You stayed!" I rush forward, throwing my arms around him. "I knew you wouldn't leave without me. Where are Mom and Mavis? Are they mad they missed their trip?"

The look on Dad's face as he peels away from me tells me everything I need to know. "Edie, it was Mom's grant. And her dream. You know that. Asking her to miss this chance..."

I swallow hard. Force a nod. "Right. I know."

And I do know. Mom met Dad when they were both studying abroad in Greece years ago. They fell in love, she got pregnant, and Mom decided to stay home with us kids and give up her career until we were older. I never really understood it. Why couldn't she do both?

When I ask Mom she'll only says she was overly worried about our safety just like any young mom. Really, though, Dad's always been the more overprotective one, while Mom is constantly pushing me to let go and embrace my wild side. I've tried to tell her I don't have a wild side, that I'm pretty sure I was born without one. That's when she gets this glint in her eye and insists that someday I'm going to surprise myself. If Mavis is around she always like to add, "In bed." Ha ha ha, Mavis.

Anyway, once I started high school, Mom decided it was time to pick up where she left off. She finished her degree and then this opportunity to work in Greece came up. Dad didn't like it. They tried to hide the fact they were arguing, but even though neither of them are screamers, there's always a certain tone to their voices when they're upset. Eventually Mom won and well, it was immediately obvious how excited she was. Suddenly Greece this and Greece that was all Mom could talk about.

So yeah, unless I was on my deathbed, there's no way Mom wasn't getting on that airplane. And Mavis, well, she was always Mom's favorite, while I've always been Dad's.

I hug Dad again. "Thank you for coming back for me."

He ruffles my hair. Or tries. It's wet, so he just sort of rubs my head instead. "Well, I had to decide who needed more help staying out of trouble—you or your mom. You won, but only just barely."

"Hey, Dad," I smile up at him. "Speaking of trouble... since we're here all summer with nothing to do, maybe you can help me get more driving practice in."

"Aw, baby girl." Dad smiles fondly. "I would rather spend an afternoon wrestling alligators than be inside a vehicle you're driving."

"Dad!"

"But I did have an idea." He rummages in his pocket and then holds up two laminated cards with a ta-da expression.

"Those are bus passes."

"Yup. Good all summer. I figured, well, maybe we could explore the public transportation system in our fair city. It's eco-friendly and it'll be an adventure!"

I stare at Dad. He is working so hard to sell this. Only the vice principal of a junior high school would be this excited about bus passes, and only a monster would burst his bubble.

"Wow. Bus passes and knitting. Best summer ever." Somehow I manage to keep most of the sarcasm out of my voice.

Dad grins back at me. "Best summer ever," he echoes. Thing is, I think he means it.

———

Keep reading for FREE! Download Fire & Flood Now!

SNEAK PEEK: THE MIDLIFE LADY'S GUIDE TO A BAD HOROSCOPE (POWERS OF THE ZODIAC #1)

1

———

I know that I'm not the first bride to be left standing at the altar with no groom in sight. It's almost a cliché — one that's always played for laughs—and usually gets them.

I'm not laughing.

But I am *smiling*, because I am Madison Thorne and Madison Thorne is always smiling. You can see it in my Facebook posts with my beautiful family, my Instagram pics with my latest to-die-for crafting idea, and in the Pinterest board of ideas I made for this special day.

Except I had always imagined that my husband would be next to me.

Okay, maybe I *am* laughing. It's a slightly hysterical giggle—there's a limit to grace under pressure. Because here's the thing: while a bride can get stood up on her wedding day by a groom with cold feet...how many women deal with a no-show husband for a vow *renewal* ceremony?

I give the minister a piece of my strained smile. We're not regular churchgoers, really, just Christmas and Easter with the family. But this minister married us twenty-five years ago and I thought it would be nice to have him perform our vow renewal, even though there's nothing religious about it. We're not even having our ceremony in a church. We're in a beautiful forest—my idea—and the spring breeze rushing past me is comforting.

Well, kind of.

About twelve years ago a cataclysmic event sent shock waves through the entire world. Natural disasters erupted everywhere, food chain supplies were broken, and it kind of felt like the apocalypse for a little bit. But the biggest shock by far was that it turned out all of the paranormal creatures we'd thought were myths were actually quite real. Vampires, werewolves, pixies, and all kinds of bizarre creatures came out of the woodwork, and it took some time for humans to adapt to the new normal.

Things were a bit hairy for a while. Some of the supes made gangs, claimed territory, and then moved on to terrorizing everyone in the vicinity. We were lucky to live in a neighborhood that was spared from the worst of it. But the church we were married in was not so fortunate. Apparently some fae fire balls went astray when they were fighting a gang of vampires. The interior of the church went up in flames, leaving only the brick shell standing. Last I heard a pack of harpy meth-heads are squatting there.

Honestly, I'm not too broken up about not being able to recreate the "I dos" we exchanged inside that dark old building. In my memories of that day, I recall feeling trapped and boxed in. I was young and powerless. It never occurred to me that I could have a say in my own destiny. Of course, it all worked out. But still, it feels good to be the one steering the ship this time.

If only I could've steered Bert's ship too, maybe he would be here right now.

With that thought, I glance over my shoulder.

Everyone I know is here…minus my husband. My parents, my kids, friends, family. And they're all looking at me with various levels of pity in their eyes. Well, no, actually, my youngest boy, Oliver, hasn't looked up from his phone. The signal out here isn't great, but I guess he doesn't need it for that shooting game he loves.

Love. Yeah. My monosyllabic son definitely loves his computer games. It's the only topic where I can get more than one-word answers from him. Once Ollie was so excited about a new skin he bought, he waxed poetic about it for a full ten minutes. I had no idea what he was talking about, but I feigned enthusiasm for his sake—after first Googling to figure out what a skin was, and hoping that my youngest wasn't wandering into some weird internet sex thing.

'Cause that's love too. Isn't it?

You take an interest in the things your loved one cares about. It's a form of showing up, even if in this instance it was only me murmuring, "Oooh," "Wow," and "Yeah, of course you should get the beheading emote."

My husband Bert is terrible at showing up in these small ways. Instead, he's the master of the grand gesture. Like a wedding renewal ceremony in front of all our friends and family.

That's how I know this is not a case of cold feet. Bert and I have been married for twenty-five years. And this whole renewal thing was his idea. He'd wanted to give me the ceremony in the woods that I'd always dreamed about—instead of the stuffy church wedding that my parents provided when I was eighteen and had a bun in the oven.

The thought of the reception dinner at the ancient firemen's hall with three hundred of our not-so-closest friends and relatives still makes me cringe. It had sticky floors and reeked of old booze and stale beer. It didn't help that I was nauseous the whole time and trying desperately to suck in my baby bump. I'd smiled through it all, though.

So here we are, in a clearing that the park service rents out for events. I had to work hard to not make it look like a summer camp pow-wow. I cleaned out the fire pit, raked all of the leaves and sticks for at least half an acre, and set up soft lighting. White Christmas lights were in the discount bin and they look lovely wound around the trees, and if a few pixies are hovering around them it just adds to the ambience. I know that particular types of supe—what people call the supernaturals—are attracted to lights, so the Christmas bulbs are doing double duty.

I even put mosquito lures in the forest in a one-mile radius so all annoying bugs would be drawn to them and leave our guests alone. As usual, I've thought of everything.

There was no sound system so I rented a generator and got the DJ set up ahead of time, all the while praying that it wouldn't rain. I got a great deal on renting a few hundred white chairs from the church, but they were a bit dingy so I got them to knock off the price if I painted them all. I even hand-stenciled a small lily onto the backrest of each one, adding a nice floral touch that can also be religious for when the chairs go back to their rightful owners.

I didn't want to spend the money on catering so I cooked everything myself, including three hundred mini cakes. Each one was hand frosted by yours truly with a heart and *Maddie & Bert* lovingly written in pink buttercream. I think I gave myself carpal tunnel—either that or I am clutching this bouquet way too hard. I force myself to relax and hope that the tension from my hands didn't go up into my smile. It needs to look natural, just like everything else out here. Everything for my perfect day.

It was worth all the work. I came in way under budget. Not that Bert gave me one. He actually specifically told me not to pinch pennies. But Bert doesn't balance the checkbook. I do. And right now...things are tight. I know it'll all turn out okay, somehow it always does. Just when it seems like we won't be able to pay the mortgage, Bert returns from Southern France—or some other equally exotic destination —with a new antique that he sells for an amount big enough to make all our dreams come true...for a while at least.

I could make one of those checks last a lifetime. But Bert's dreams are too big. And expensive. He says that's why we make a perfect team. His head is in the clouds while my feet are on the ground. And he's right; we've gone through twenty-five years this way. It's just that sometimes...

With a sigh, I lift my head to the sky, it's clear and the full moon hangs low, visible even though night is hours away. Someone was telling me something about this moon...it was a blood moon or something. I can't remember. Maybe tonight after the guests leave and it's just me and Bert we can turn off all the lights and lay under the night sky to stargaze...and then maybe direct our attention elsewhere.

Beside me, the minister clears his throat. The last twenty-five years haven't been kind to him; he needs a cane to stay upright and is looking deeply uncomfortable. "It's been thirty-five minutes..." he tells me. His tone is apologetic, but there's an edge that wasn't in his voice when we first realized that Bert was missing. Then he said, "Renewal ceremonies are such joyous occasions. Like so many of the best things in life, they're worth waiting for." I guess, like everyone, the minister has limits.

"Just five more minutes," I say. The same as I've said six

times now. I hope my smile still looks genuine, and I'm not showing too many teeth. Even if I did have them whitened just for the occasion.

His lips compress, but then he nods. I know that I won't get another five minutes after this. If Bert doesn't show soon this minister will be walking—or, em, shuffling—away.

Darn it, Bert!

I smooth down my dress—a beautiful retro piece from the seventies that I found at a garage sale while looking for the vintage clothing shop—and sigh once more.

My Bert. I've told him so many times that he packs his days too full. He's a man who is hungry for life. He wants to experience everything. It's what I love about him. But also, after twenty plus years, it's what leads to most of my frustrations with him. He's never on time, dashing in at the last possible minute for parent-teacher conferences. Or showing up fashionably late to parties being thrown in our own backyard. Once he was in charge of bringing the welcome bags, and showed up just in time to give them to guests as they were leaving.

And it's not that he forgets. It's always, "I'm sorry baby, I got hung up..."

He's a businessman. Always making deals, meeting new people, cementing old friendships, and then selling something to them. And he financially supports our family—as he reminds me more often than is altogether necessary. There's a little flare of anger in my stomach at the thought, and I have to work hard to keep my smile in place. The minister clears his throat and I know it's time to get this party started—without the groom.

Unlike the first time around, this is *my day*. And nothing —not even my husband—is going to ruin it for me.

I turn to face my family and friends. "We all know Bert;

he probably spotted a piece of artwork in the airport that is worth more than anyone ever thought, and is currently haggling with the art director—who will be his new best friend after some drinks. So let's go ahead and celebrate, and we can do the ceremony later!" I say, with a huge smile.

There is a collective sigh of relief. I make sure the minister gets a chair so he can rest, give a wave to the DJ to let him know to start spinning, and put the fairy lights on twinkle mode, which brings in a few more pixies and makes for a festive atmosphere. I assure everyone that I'm fine; it's just an unexpected delay. I move from group to group, smiling like my life depends on it.

I read once that a scientific study showed that the physical act of smiling can actually help lift a person's mood. Now, though, I have to wonder exactly how they knew this. I'd lie through my upturned lips that this is a perfect day and that my every smile only increases my joy. And if they called me on it, I'd only smile harder.

"Mom, are you okay?" my oldest, Nathan, asks. How am I old enough to have a twenty-four-year old child?! He's already in grad school. An actual adult. I am old enough to have three adult children. Even number four, the baby, is now in high school! Nathan sees the stricken look on my face and misunderstands—he thinks I'm upset with his father. And of course I'm not. Of course I'm not mad at Bert. Of course not.

"Yes, you know your father," I say with a wave of my hand.

"He doesn't deserve you," he mumbles. "He takes you for granted." My heart twists for my little boy, even if he is all grown up now. Once he worshipped the ground Bert walked on. But too many years of missed baseball games, debate finals, and even his college graduation has put a strain on their relationship. I make a note to have Bert invite him for a guy's night out. They'll have some drinks together and Bert will smooth things over until Nathan forgets all about those old hurts. Well...mostly.

"Marriage is work," I tell him, giving his arm a little squeeze. "You'll understand one day."

"Sure. Mom, get some food," he says. But I probably won't. There's a feeling in my stomach that doesn't mix well with food. Disappointment. My face still apparently isn't doing a great job of conveying absolute joy, because Nathan's glower deepens.

I decide it's time to change the subject. "Do you know who that man is over there?" I point to a tall dark-haired man who slipped into the party late. Irrationally, I'm a bit annoyed at this stranger—not for crashing my party, but for giving me a moment's hope that Bert had finally arrived.

Nathan frowns. "I saw Aunt Stephy hanging on him earlier..." he says.

"Oh, okay,"I say, since that pretty much answers it all.

My younger sister Stephanie is a triple divorcée on the hunt for number four. Which is fine. To each their own. I'm not here to judge her choices. But it's a bit annoying that she refuses to extend the same courtesy to me. She's made it very clear that she thinks this whole vow renewal ceremony is lame and cheesy and—worst of all—smug.

Well, I bet she's loving how things turned out. There's nothing to be smug about now.

Again, Nathan must see something of what I'm thinking, because he curls his hands into fists. "When Dad shows up I'm going to..."

"You won't do anything," I cut him off. "You won't ruin the party."

"Dad already did that," he shoots back, but he won't

cause a fuss. He knows I would hate that. Any type of confrontation is absolutely not my thing. Bert likes to talk about how we never fight. Ever. He does a whole little bit about it when we meet new people.

"This is my wife, Maddie," he says, a twinkle in his eyes. "I know the name paired with that wild curly hair of hers makes her look like a lady with a temper. But believe it or not, we've never had a single fight. And it's not because I'm a perfect saint either. Or no, I could *tempt* a saint." He pauses here for knowing laughter from those familiar with him— and almost everyone is. Then he continues, "But my Maddie here, she never gets mad."

Then it's my turn to give the punchline, "I never get mad, but someday I might get even."

Every single time Bert reacts like it's his first time hearing it. His eyes pop wide and he startles back, a hand to his heart. "Uh-oh," he cries as the laughter around us grows louder. "I better watch myself then!'

I always laugh along. But I have to say, I've noticed that he never joins in. Instead, he smiles and takes a drink, always surveying those around us to make sure he's doing his job of making everyone like him. Sometimes when I see him reading the room like that it sends a chill up my spine...and not always a good one. He always knows how to get exactly the right reaction out of people, and how to get what he wants from them. Lord knows he's got me. Smiling, Maddie "Never Mad" Thorne.

But really this might be the last straw. Maybe this time I won't shove my feelings down. Maybe this time I'll curse him out and threaten to...

I don't know what I'd do. I've put so much work into being perfectly nice that I don't even know how to get angry. And it's not like I could ever throw something at Bert, stamp my foot and demand an apology—I've never had to. He always walks in the door with the right words, and I can't resist a man who isn't afraid to say he's sorry.

I've loved Robert Thorne for as long as I can remember.

"Mom!" the twins call to me. "Come dance!"

I plaster on a smile and go to them. They are a perfectly adorable pair, with matching faces that somehow look great on both a boy and a girl. In family pictures we always look fantastic, even if Bert is sometimes a little flushed from running into the studio fifteen minutes behind schedule.

The music is lovely as it bounces off the trees and flows through the evening air, the pixies bobbing up and down along with it. It's getting darker, and we'll have to pay some attention to make sure there aren't any harpies or vampires lurking in the higher branches of the trees, but the park service does a pretty good job of keeping public areas free of some of the more violent supes. In fact, I had raided the cash register at my vintage clothing store to slip the rangers a few extra twenties to keep them on the party perimeter after sunset, just in case.

I had a plan, and I wasn't going to let anything ruin my perfect night.

But I didn't plan on my husband being a no-show.

Continue reading **The Midlife Lady's Guide to a Bad Horoscope!**

him even though interspecies dating is taboo. I think he might like me too...even though I did accidentally set him on fire the first time we met. Awkward!

It's not all fun and games, though. MOA has a darker side and the more time I spend here, the more secrets I uncover. And the worst secret of all just might be about me.

Fire & Flood is a young adult magic academy fantasy novel with non-stop action. It contains a spunky heroine, one best friend with the gift of sight...to see tomorrow's lunch menu, a mean-girl vampire roommate with a carnivorous plant, and a meet-cute with her roommate's hot twin brother that almost kills them both.

Read the first book for FREE!

———

Three women experience their midlife crisis in the worst way - by finding out they are all married to the same man.

Their shared husband deals with magical artifacts, and has hidden three pieces of a *talentum dei* - a magical object that can deliver the powers of a god to its handler - with each of his wives. When the three women accidentally meet and the *talentum* assembles, they are each given a power that matches their star sign, and their husband - intent on having power for himself - makes a grab for the *talentum*, only to have it kill him. The three - very different - women find themselves imbued with powers, suddenly single, and on the run from powerful people who are after the *talentum*... with the ghost of their shared dead husband along for the ride.

The Midlife Lady's Guide to a Bad Horoscope is available now!

ABOUT THE AUTHORS

DEMITRIA LUNETTA is the author of the YA books THE FADE, BAD BLOOD, and the sci-fi duology, IN THE AFTER and IN THE END. She is also an editor and contributing author for the YA anthology, AMONG THE SHADOWS: 13 STORIES OF DARKNESS & LIGHT. Find her at www.demitrialunetta.com for news on upcoming projects and releases.

KATE KARYUS QUINN is an avid reader and menthol chapstick addict with a BFA in theater and an MFA in film and television production. She lives in Buffalo, New York with her husband, three children, and one enormous dog. She has three young adult novels published with HarperTeen: ANOTHER LITTLE PIECE, (DON'T YOU) FORGET ABOUT ME, AND DOWN WITH THE SHINE. She also recently released her first adult novel, THE SHOW MUST GO ON, a romantic comedy. Find out more at www.katekaryusquinn.com

MARLEY LYNN is a lost child of the gods, who waits on the shores of Lake Erie for her parents to bring her home. In the meantime, she contents herself with reading, writing, and gardening. Find out more at www.MarleyLynn.com

ACKNOWLEDGMENTS

Thank you to Marin McGinnis for taking care of our copy edits!

And, of course, a big thank you to our families for putting up with us crazy writers.